THE COLOUR OF RAIN

ff

EMMA TENNANT

The Colour of Rain

faber and faber

LONDON · BOSTON

First published in 1963
under the pseudonym Catherine Aydy
by Weidenfeld and Nicolson
This paperback reissued in 1988
by Faber and Faber Limited
3 Queen Square London WC1N 3AU
Reprinted 1988

Photoset by Wilmaset Birkenhead Wirral
Printed in Great Britain by
Richard Clay Ltd, Bungay, Suffolk
All rights reserved

British Library Cataloguing in Publication Data

Tennant, Emma
The colour of rain
I. Title
823'.914 [F]   PR6070.E52
ISBN 0-571-15017-9

FOR TEDDY

The Colour of Rain was written in 1962 and published by Weidenfeld and Nicolson the following year with a cover by Osbert Lancaster. The cover depicted a scene of well-to-do young marrieds and their nannies, wheeling prams. The spikes were on the heels of the employers rather than on their heads – these were surmounted by a stiff beehive, lacquered to the sheen of Mycenaean gold – but the odd headscarf or inane smile suggested a *milieu* which would soon, like that ancient civilization, be swallowed up and disappear under the hordes of student radicals, hippie Dylan-wailers and a monstrous regiment of women with hair as flat as Cromwell's. Once the sixties began in earnest, or so it was thought, these strange, anachronistic persons would exist no longer, their conversations likely to be blown away for ever by the changing wind.

The novel, written almost entirely in dialogue, was intended as a sort of *'hommage'* to Henry Green; and while it in no way comes near the achievements of that brilliant comic and poetic writer, thinking of his work as I wrote (I was in my early twenties) helped me to structure the book and to bring off a social comedy with some economy. I wrote the book under a pseudonym – Catherine Aydy – again in imitation of Green, whose real name was not Green. But beyond that point it cannot be said that there was any similarity in the reception of the *œuvre*. For – mistakenly, I believe – the publishers submitted *The Colour of Rain* for the Prix Formentor, a classy literary event held in Majorca. There, I was told, the novel was held aloft by the Chairman of the Judges, the distinguished author Alberto Moravia, who denounced it as an example of the decadence of the contemporary British novel. Some reports have it that the book was then hurled into a wastepaper basket; but this has never been authenticated.

The Colour of Rain, therefore, had a short and turbulent life. Its title is perhaps misleading, suggesting a prose poem rather than an attempt at a description of a small band of people and their inherited assumptions about the world and their place in it. Yet the 'sameness', the 'nothing-happened-ness' of these lives can, obviously, be supported only by money and a large domestic labour force. The trick is not to show the wires – to suggest that this sophisticated and enviable *train de vie* is held up by nothing at all. And that is the definition of the colour of rain: nothing. Nothing at all.

Emma Tennant, 1987

CHAPTER ONE

A big children's party was in progress. Alice was late, she thought, in collecting her four, but screams and thumping from upstairs showed that the conjuror was going on a little longer than usual. She left her coat in the hall and ran up the narrow stairs to the first floor. The drawing-room door stood open. 'Who's that?' a voice called out easily from inside. 'Oh, it's you, Alice. How lovely to see you.'

A girl got up from the sofa and presented a cheek to be kissed. Alice kissed it and threw herself with abandon into an armchair. 'I really thought I'd find that everyone had gone. It must be a wonderful party to go on so long.'

'Well, it's been as good as one could hope for in this house. Your house is so enormous and exciting, Alice. The children adore your parties, especially the fancy dress ones.' There was a short silence.

Both young women looked intently round the room. 'I never properly noticed the material on the walls,' Alice confided in a slightly subdued voice. 'It's a sort of velvet, isn't it?'

'It is velvet.'

1

'Oh.'

'I expect it's just got a little shabby after all these years. Actually,' the girl ran on, 'I still don't see why it's got that worn look. It's not as if it had been sitting down.'

Alice laughed. 'That horrid beastly worn look. I do know what you mean.'

'Do you realize that Evvy's back from wherever it was he went? We must all do something for him.'

Alice blushed very faintly. 'Oh, Ruth, what fun. Of course we must. He's been gone for such ages. Where is he staying?'

'With us.'

Ruth's moment of triumph was thoroughly spoiled by the door opening and a small plump woman running in. 'It's awful,' she gasped, 'I went right upstairs by mistake and found myself in the middle of the party. One of the nannies asked me whose nanny I was. So I said I was a mother, and it somehow seemed disgraceful.' She gave a loud shouting laugh. Both Ruth and Alice recoiled, then exchanged glances and laughed themselves. 'But has Caspian been good, Ruth?' she gazed with cheerful mock anxiety at her friend.

'Absolutely exemplary.' At the same time Ruth brushed the question aside and crossed the room to the drink tray which stood on a small japanned table in the 'L' of the room. 'Have something, Sylvie. Vodka, gin, whisky?'

'Gosh, I really would rather like one. What about you, Alice?'

'Oh I can't,' said Alice, who seemed to have slipped into some kind of trance by the crackling fire, 'but you go on, Sylvie. You must need one after driving in this traffic.'

Finally they all three sipped at glasses of Dubonnet tightly packed with ice. Sylvie arranged her possessions around her on the floor with care – cigarettes, matches and drink – and then leant back with a sigh of contentment. 'I hear that Evvy's staying here.' She could hardly prevent herself from sounding bright. 'Is he likely to come in before we go?'

'One never knows.' Ruth gave a fond proprietary smile. 'I hope so anyway.'

A soft tap at the door heralded the entrance of Alice's nanny.

'I'm sorry Mrs Green, but I thought maybe it was bedtime.' She cocked her head to one side.

'Yes, yes, of course. Get their coats on, Nanny. We must go, Ruth, but see you on Monday, I hope.'

'You'll miss Elizabeth, what a shame.' Ruth glanced vaguely at the everpresent nanny. 'Send them home in a taxi, Alice, why don't you? There are plenty outside.'

'I can drop them on the way,' Sylvie gallantly offered. 'After all I have to drive half-way across London, so what difference can it make?'

The nanny visibly brightened. 'Oh, I can't see why not,' Alice laughed. 'Yes Nanny, Mrs Lamont will drive you home. I don't feel in the slightest like leaving. Good-bye, Sylvie. You're an angel.'

3

Suddenly Sylvie had been despatched and the two friends settled down with a more conspiratorial air in their former seats.

'What are you doing tonight?' Ruth enquired casually.

'Just at home with Robert. What about you, I suppose you're going out to play bridge again?' her companion teased.

'Well, it's hardly my fault.' Ruth seemed annoyed. 'It's Robin that loves playing so much. Better than denying him it, I can tell you.' Unmentionable consequences suggested themselves.

'But it's better than us,' Alice consoled her. 'Robert hates going out, it's a struggle to get him to leave the house.'

Ruth gave a sympathetic sigh.

'Why on earth did we ever marry, I wonder?' As if to answer her question she rose and consulted the long Chippendale glass. A small satisfied face looked back at her and in the distance Alice's beauty was reflected, the colour heightened by the flames of the fire.

'You really are in good looks at the moment, Alice. Evvy said he was longing to see you.'

'I can't think why he's not staying with me,' Alice admitted.

Ruth looked upset. 'I know it's not anything like so comfortable here but I did write to him and make him promise to come. The poor thing probably felt he couldn't refuse.' She seemed to be on the point of tossing her head and walked again over to the drinks tray instead.

'I'll switch to gin as well, I think,' Alice cried. 'No, it's got nothing to do with it being more comfortable at home – and it isn't anyway – it's the loveliness of having Evvy in the house that I shall miss. The mornings, you know.'

'Sitting on one's bed in the morning? Yes, isn't that heavenly. Evvy's dressing-gowns are always so beautiful.' Ruth shut her eyes and rocked for a little while back and forth.

'After Robert's vile horrible dressing-gown . . . and telephoning with Evvy is such fun. I do envy you, Ruth.' The girls looked at each other in complete sympathy.

'But what are you planning for Monday?' Ruth relentlessly asked.

'I must have a new combination of people – '

'Oh how exciting – are you going to ask – '

'So I thought – '

They were interrupted by a low buzzing sound from the telephone. Ruth snatched the receiver impatiently. 'Yes, what is it? What? Well, show her up. Really,' she went on, slightly breathless, 'that Spanish man is quite hopeless, you know. Elizabeth has arrived and is downstairs and José didn't know what to do with her.'

'That would happen to Elizabeth,' said Alice, laughing. 'She'll think that's all you can expect if you don't have real servants.'

'And she's right,' said Ruth, still heated. 'It's true,

though, Alice; let's see if she says something marvellous or not.'

They were almost taken unawares by their friend, who had opened the door and was beside them in a flash. 'I'm so late that I know I've missed the children. But I wanted frightfully to see the new room downstairs. Can I?'

Elizabeth Murray was a tall girl with the striking good looks of a model, which in fact she had been before her marriage. She had a curious way of holding herself, half as if she wanted to show off her appearance and half as if she wanted to deprecate it. Thus she stood in front of Ruth and Alice.

'What a terribly pretty suit,' Ruth said a little falsely. 'Does it come from here?'

'Not actually,' said Elizabeth, who seemed tenser than usual today. 'No, it comes from Paris.'

Alice caught Ruth's eye but they both looked disappointed.

'I thought it must,' said Ruth, suppressing a giggle.

'I adore the fittings really,' Elizabeth went on. 'Have you ever been to – well to one of the houses? One can go over for the day and have a tremendous lunch at La Perouse or somewhere and then have a fitting and then fly home. And be in time for dinner.' She laughed.

'You know perfectly well that I haven't ever had anything from there,' Ruth said sternly. She glanced at Alice. 'Are you sure you really want to see the downstairs room, Elizabeth? Because I've got to start thinking about getting ready for dinner fairly soon.'

'Oh, are you going out?' Elizabeth said, sounding surprised. 'Anywhere nice?'

'Only the Becks,' said Ruth, who was by now cross with herself.

'How lovely. But are you sure you can face showing it to me? What about another time? Heavens, it's much later than I thought and I really ought to get home or I'll – '

'I've been longing to hear what you thought about it,' Ruth cried.

'I'll come down with you,' Alice suddenly said, 'and get my coat on the way.'

'Oh good. I've already heard so much about it that I'm quite excited,' Elizabeth maintained.

The small downstairs room was dimly lit and appeared to the visitors to be upholstered in sackcloth. Two abstract pictures were discernible.

'God, what a wonderful idea,' both the girls cried.

'No I mean it, it's so simple and bare which is such a relief,' Elizabeth added.

'But the point is for it eventually not to be bare,' cried poor Ruth. 'When I can afford to buy more pictures I'll hang them in here. Evvy's telling me what to buy.'

'I must go, Ruth,' said Alice in a stage whisper as Elizabeth stood in silent contemplation before one of the paintings.

'Oh, so must I,' Elizabeth said hurriedly. She kissed Ruth. 'I think it's absolutely lovely. It's so irritating that we can't have a room like this in either house because of every inch being panelled. I do envy you.'

'I know, it's the same in Montpelier Square,' Alice said as if she had just realized it. 'See you on Monday, Ruth, and do tell Evvy to ring me when he gets in.' The girls strolled to the front door. Their cars were parked just around the corner in Pelham Crescent.

'Isn't it odd,' Elizabeth confided to Alice, 'that the minute one leaves Ruth one forgets her altogether?'

'Ohhh,' cooed Alice, sounding like a dove, 'I do love her. But I suppose you're right. You are clever Elizabeth. I'll see you on Monday anyway.'

'How simply lovely. I can't wait. About 8.30?'

'Try and make it a little earlier,' Alice confessed as they separated and found their cars.

'I do know what you mean,' Elizabeth called after her. 'Pont's always making a scene about starting dinner late.' Her words were wafted away into the square gardens where they were caught by a tramp.

'Damn her bloody butler,' Alice swore as she drove down the Fulham Road.

CHAPTER TWO

The house in Montpelier Square was very magnificent. It was really two houses joined together and had six windows across the front. Two tubs of geraniums stood either side of the ancient front door in a small paved garden. Out at the back was a long lawn and a collection of old trees, but not very many flowers. Alice threw off her coat in the hall and went into the library. Here a thin bookcase contained some bound books; otherwise the panelled walls had been painted white and the only touch of colour to be found was in the scarlet curtains. Robert was sitting on the sofa reading the *Evening Standard*.

'Hullo-o,' said Alice.

'Well hullo,' Robert exclaimed.

'Did you see the children when they came in?'

'Yes – for a minute.'

'Oh good. I never really trust Sylvie driving,' said Alice, relieved.

'Sylvie brought them back, did she?' Robert sounded amused. 'Where from?'

'Oh, from tea with Ruth.'

'And how's Ruth?'

'Much the same I suppose. I hope she makes a little more effort when she comes to dinner on Monday. Last time she hardly spoke at all. I really felt quite cross with her.'

'It's because Robin talks too much I expect,' Robert said in a wise tone. 'You always seem to have plenty to say to her on the telephone, though.'

'Well, obviously that's different,' Alice replied. 'Did you have a good day?' She opened her bag and took out a small nail-file which she looked at and then popped back.

'Yes – fine.'

A man appeared in the doorway and said, 'Dinner is served.'

'Thank you, Mario,' Alice said. They went into the dining-room and sat at either end of a long mahogany table. The servant handed them Heinz tomato soup in a china tureen. This was followed by sausages and mash. Robert looked displeased. 'Where's the Worcester sauce?' he demanded.

'It's on the sideboard – I'll get it, there's no point in ringing for Mario.' Alice ran over to pick up the bottle. 'Could we open one of those half-bottles of wine, do you think?'

Robert was surprised. 'Of course, if you want some. But why hasn't Mario put it out?'

'He doesn't know about that sort of thing, Robert. He isn't a real servant, you know.'

'What do you mean – a real servant? We pay him enough, don't we?'

10

'Not as much as real servants cost,' said Alice firmly. 'You know what Elizabeth pays Pont?'

'Who's Pont? No, honestly, Alice, I don't think it's worth discussing. I don't really see why we need Mario. Anyway, I'll get you some wine.'

Every time he got up he looked shorter to Alice than she had expected. This was perhaps because he had a very large head and splendid body fitted on to small and sturdy legs. When he came back he opened the half-bottle and Alice sipped at her glass with pleasure.

'Elizabeth is so ridiculous,' she said. 'It's all so pretentious somehow. I'm very glad we don't live in their house; it's much too decorated. And painting the drawing-room yellow has made it so dark. As a matter of fact it's taken this house over a year to recover from being painted. I felt that it hated it and was furious.'

Robert smiled. 'Have we really been in this house as long as a year?'

'Why?' Does it feel much less?' Alice asked.

'Oh, I don't know – longer perhaps.'

Alice took another glass of wine and lit a cigarette. 'Being married to Elizabeth must be expensive,' she remarked.

'Old Tom can afford it. Well, dinner's over, isn't it?'

'I do love sitting a long time with the coffee and things,' Alice murmured. Robert did not hear her and walked through into the library where he made straight for a large hi-fi set built into the wall. Alice

11

blew out the short candles in their silver candle-sticks.

'Do you remember when your father gave us these?' she called into the other room. A crescendo of noise was the answer.

'I think it sounds best like this,' Robert cried, and appeared in the doorway a little red in the face from stooping over his precious equipment. 'Don't you, Alp?'

'I think it sounds marvellous. Oh, it's Camelot, isn't it? I do wish it would come over here,' Alice settled herself appreciatively on the sofa.

'But what I really want to hear most is my African record on this machine.' He expertly changed the records in mid-stream and at the press of a button a little spurt of water sprang forth to cleanse the old one. The room was filled with the eerie noise of drumbeats bursting out from the loudspeakers concealed behind the bookcase and under the windowsills.

'That horrid African record,' Alice said.

Robert turned down the volume very slightly. 'How are the children doing at school?' he yelled.

Alice gave a nod which reassured him.

'I'm for bed,' Alice said and yawned. Robert nodded vigorously and knelt once again by the gramophone. 'I just want to switch on the tape-recording apparatus and listen to the poetry that Luke and I read into it the other night when you went out.'

'Ah, I knew that I shouldn't go out and leave you

12

with Luke,' Alice said in a scolding voice. 'Whatever did you get up to?'

'Just the usual sort of thing,' said Robert, sounding pleased. By now Alice had reached the door. Her bag swung open and she absentmindedly fastened it. Two rather blurred voices reciting a poem in a foreign language came from the loudspeakers. Alice gave another great yawn and went up the small staircase to bed.

'I thought I'd lunch with Alice today,' Evvy said, 'but she doesn't know it yet.' He was telephoning from Ruth's bed and lay sprawled across the pillows with his head resting lightly on her shoulder. Ruth stared at him sideways, almost rigid with the effort not to disturb him. She looked down in distaste at her crumpled lacy nightdress and hoped that he hadn't noticed its unfresh appearance. Evvy had come into her room that morning before Robin had left for the office, an unprecedented occurence due to Evvy's desire to get on the telephone early and Robin's unusual lateness. Now Robin had gone, although not before losing his briefcase and eventually finding it in the folds of Evvy's dressing-gown.

'Oh good, because I'm lunching with Alice today,' said Sylvie on the other end of the wire, 'why don't we meet first and go there together?' Ruth gave Evvy's shoulder a slight nudge. 'Oh, I can't do that,' Evvy said. 'Ruth and I have got some shopping to do. But I'll see you there – how are you, darling?'

'I can't really tell you now,' Sylvie's voice said mysteriously.

'You're always so brisk and busy,' Evvy complained. 'It's wonderful, I suppose. Isn't it, Ruth?'

'I must ring off,' the voice said with determination. 'Can't wait to see you.' There was a click.

'Who do you want to ring now?' Ruth asked drowsily.

'I want to talk to you. How have you been getting on?'

'Oh Evvy – it's so hard to explain when one feels that everything isn't going quite – '

'I want to know all about Alice and the house. And she and Robert? Just the same?'

Ruth stared at Evvy a long time before answering. He was one of the most faultless young men imaginable. Long doe's eyes of soft brown were most of the time half veiled by lashes of an amazing length. A sulky but undeniably beautiful mouth provided the expression in too classical a face which was rescued again by a cloud of soft dark hair and a romantic haggardness. She sighed almost inaudibly and said:

'I don't know what you're going to think of the house, Evvy. Alice hasn't done anything to it since you were last here.'

'You mean they still don't sit in the drawing-room?' Evvy sat upright on the bed.

'I knew you'd be shocked.' Ruth laughed. 'She

14

absolutely adores the house, of course, but one would think she didn't care.'

'But doesn't Robert give her any money for it? He's so rich, it's quite ridiculous.'

'I think he's incredibly mean. But Alice never talks about it – if she cared one would think she would complain.'

'She really is odd,' Evvy mused.

'Come on, we must get up,' Ruth said rather sharply. 'Let's go to the antique shops in the Fulham Road this morning. It's so nice and near home.'

Evvy laughed and pulled himself up to his thin height. 'You are a little provincial these days,' he teased her.

'But they're the best shops,' said Ruth, stung.

'I know, darling. I'll see you downstairs in an hour then.'

'You do take ages to get up,' Ruth began, then sighed again as he sauntered out of the room. 'All right, Evvy.'

'How was Ruth?' Alice wanted to know as she tried to extricate the spoon from the lobster mousse that Mario held just slightly out of her reach. 'Did you have a good morning?'

'She needs a few lessons in taste,' Evvy said indistinctly, for his teeth were also finding difficulty in coping with the mousse. 'Some of the things she wanted to buy were quite *extraordinaire*.'

15

Sylvie shouted with laughter. 'Ruth does have some odd ideas I know. You must help her, Evvy.'

'Oh, I shall. But what's been going on here, Alice darling? You don't seem to have made much progress with the house.'

'Oh, don't be difficult, Evvy. You know I can't have real houses like other people,' said Alice, looking quite lovely.

'Of course you can, darling. You just need some *objets* and you really must have flowers. Otherwise – a beautiful house like this – well, it makes it so bleak.'

'But what about furniture for the drawing-room?' Alice wailed. 'I'll never be able to do it.'

'Of course you will,' Evvy comforted her. 'Isn't Robert interested?'

'Oh – I don't know, honestly Evvy, I'd rather we didn't . . .'

'I suppose one's lucky having nothing but horrible modern things,' Sylvie said cheerfully.

'Oh, I don't think so, darling,' Evvy said.

A large dish of kedgeree was carried into the room. 'I am so sorry that the food's so awful,' Alice cried. 'I didn't know you were coming until the last minute, Evvy.'

'What on earth is it?' Evvy asked with a bewitching smile.

'You must know what it is,' Sylvie said. 'After all, Evvy, you are English really. You can't have forgotten every single thing about England just because you don't live here.'

'I have,' Evvy replied, this time glancing keenly at Alice. She blushed.

'Do promise that you'll stay with me as usual when you next come,' she begged him. 'I think it's very disloyal of you to stay with Ruth.'

'But she wrote and wrote,' he said, blushing too.

'Any news about Judith?' Sylvie intercepted their exchange of glances.

'Oh, yes,' Evvy looked interested, 'is she behaving as outrageously as ever?'

'Very much so,' Alice answered in a prim tone. 'She's got another lover.'

'What? A husband and two lovers? How on earth does she do it?' Evvy cried. 'Who's the new one?'

'Mark Guest.'

'Good heavens – one never knows anything if one lives à l'étranger.'

'How long has it been going on?'

'Oh, a month or two,' Sylvie said in a matter-of-fact voice.

'It really is a little too squalid,' Evvy said thoughtfully.

'I can't think how she does it,' Alice said. 'And see so much of her children. And give those enormous dinner parties.'

'It's just energy,' Sylvie explained. 'The lucky thing.'

'Sylvie darling, you're absolutely full of energy,' said Evvy. 'I remember, before my illness, how I used to be able to do anything I wanted. It's so hard these days to have to realize that one can't.'

17

'But how is your horrid illness?' Alice cried. 'Oh Evvy, I never asked you properly about it.'

'I just have to be careful not to do too much,' Evvy answered. 'I shouldn't really drink, you know.'

'What delicious fruit salad,' Sylvie said.

'There's one thing,' Alice confided, 'that Judith did tell me the other day. She told me she went to a marvellous astrologer called Mrs Clare. Have you heard of her, Evvy?'

'How could I have?' Evvy said gloomily, 'when I'm almost never here.'

'Well, you're the one person that might have,' Alice replied. 'You know all those fascinating fortune-tellers in Paris and Rome.'

A tin of Nescafé and a china jug of boiling water were placed in front of Alice. Evvy looked at his wristwatch.

'I've got hundreds of things to do this afternoon, but why don't we look in and see her for a few minutes? I want to know what my health is going to be like in London. It's always so bad here; the flora and fauna here don't agree with me.'

'Oh, I'm sure they could,' Sylvia cried.

Evvy still stared at Alice, who was stirring the coffee powder into the water.

'All right, let's,' she said. 'But I always think that it's all very frightening. What a shame you can't come, Sylvie.'

'Well I suppose I could if I took the children to the pantomime tomorrow instead – '

'Oh, you mustn't do that to your children,' Evvy said firmly.

'No, I suppose I mustn't,' Sylvie agreed.

They all three got up and went into the library.

'I know you think I'm very naughty not having any pictures in here,' Alice said. 'But I don't know what to get. What do you think would look nice in here, Evvy?'

'Oh, almost anything,' Evvy answered in a bored voice. 'Look, Alice, I think we must go and see Mrs Clare now. I feel it's the right moment.'

'Well, I must be off,' Sylvie said bravely. 'Evvy, when am I going to see you?'

'I'll tell you what, Sylvie,' he answered. 'I'll paint a mural for you in your vile modern house, if you like.'

'Of course I like,' Sylvie cried. 'And think what a lovely lot of you I'll see. And we could give a party for its opening. How terrific.'

'A *vernissage*,' Evvy murmured. 'Hurry up, Alice, darling. We're leaving.'

'You are in a bossy mood today,' Alice said, smiling, as they left the house.

19

CHAPTER THREE

'And you can't remember the exact hour of your birth?' Mrs Clare said.

'No, I'm sure it was at three thirty in the morning,' said Alice staunchly. 'I really can remember my mother telling me, Mrs Clare.'

Evvy sat outside, having already had his interview. There had been no time for him to tell Alice of the outcome before Mrs Clare had called her in.

'Well, I see a great change in your life – and fairly soon,' said Mrs Clare. It was rather dark and she appeared to be having some difficulty in reading Alice's chart. The lighted bedroom windows of the Connaught Hotel opposite slightly illuminated the room through the net curtains.

'The lighting in here's so bad,' Mrs Clare continued.

'What sort of change do you see?' Alice prompted her.

'Oh, yes. Well, a complete change, you know, my dear. Are you married?'

'Yes.'

'Then I think that your husband's going to be sent

abroad by his work. And you'll go with him, of course. I definitely see life in a foreign country. Do you like that?'

Alice paused. 'Yes, I think I do,' she said slowly.

'And a lot of different friends – oh yes, I see plenty of them. You won't know yourself in a year's time. Is it likely that your husband might be sent abroad?'

'I suppose so,' Alice said dubiously.

'I won't say that I can't see a love affair in your life in the near future, my dear, because I can. But I want to warn you that it will bring great sorrow.'

'Oh dear, and I haven't started on it at this moment?' Alice agitatedly asked.

'No, not yet. That's definite. It's something in the future. A handsome fellow, too – if you can possibly avoid it I must advise you to do so.'

'Why, what will happen?' said Alice, trying to remain calm.

'Oh, he'll love you all right, never you worry. But he'll become very ill. There's a strong possibility here that you'll lose him altogether. It's my duty to tell you that.'

'I'm very glad you did,' Alice said gratefully. 'How will I recognize him?'

'You just will, my dear,' Mrs Clare said dreamily. Don't forget I told you that you will lose him through some horrible accident, perhaps, and not through any cooling off, as they call it, on his part. That's the trouble with you Librans,' she continued as she showed Alice to the door. 'Everything fine on the home front and endless troubles in love. It's because you're searching for your equilibrium the whole time, did you know that?'

'No, I didn't,' Alice admitted. 'Oh, I forgot to tell you who sent us here, Mrs Clare. It was Mrs Defoe.'

'Ah, Judith,' Mrs Clare said familiarly. 'Yes, she comes to me quite often. There's a chart for you.'

'Why, what's in it?' Alice was eager to know.

'She's got a very full house,' Mrs Clare confided in her. 'But there are various planets about to enter yours at any moment now,' she went on. 'Just be careful, that's all you must bear in mind. Could you be kind enough to write the cheque out to cash?'

Out in the passage Evvy was lurking impatiently. 'Let's have some tea at the Connaught and *discuter*,' he suggested.

'Very well, but I'll miss the children's bedtime,' Alice complained.

'It won't take long.' He hurried her across the road. 'I must say, that woman is either a genius or she's mad,' Evvy said as they ordered tea and toast and butter.

'Why? Did she tell you about your disease?' Alice demanded of him.

'Oh, she hardly mentioned that,' Evvy said airily. 'She told me I was going to have a love affair with someone that would change my whole life.'

'Did she really?' said Alice, very interested. 'How did she say it would end?' she added, crossing her fingers under the table.

'She didn't actually say,' Evvy admitted cheerfully. 'What did she say about you, darling?'

'The most horrible things,' Alice said in a low voice. 'She said my whole life was going to change. But do you think she meant Alberto when she talked about your love affair, Evvy darling?'

'No, I don't see why she should have meant that,' Evvy said huffily. 'The toast here is really quite good,' he added in a more hopeful voice.

'Yes, it's not too bad,' Alice agreed. 'But actually, Mrs Clare said that I was going to spend the rest of my life abroad.'

'The rest of your life?' Evvy demanded incredulously.

'Well, more or less,' Alice said, fidgeting.

'How very curious,' Evvy said remotely.

'I mean, Robert's hardly likely to be sent there – anywhere – is he?'

'I shouldn't have thought so.'

They finished their tea in silence.

'What a relief to have a *thé anglais* once in a while,' Evvy remarked, as they waited for a taxi on the steps of the Connaught. 'Because I shall have to get back soon.'

'What, to Lisbon?' Alice cried. 'But Evvy, you've only just come.'

'Oh, not to Lisbon,' Evvy said impatiently, 'I've got to go to Beirut by the end of the month.'

'What on earth for?'

'My sister – you remember Dolly? – well, she's going to be out there and it's far too long since I've seen her. So I'll join her there.'

23

'Beirut, how lovely,' Alice said wistfully. 'That must be rather near Greece isn't it?'

'Yes of course, why, are you going to be there? What a lovely idea if we were there together. You'd adore Dolly actually.'

'Well, John thought of going on one of those cruises rather soon – not over Christmas obviously – perhaps even before, and I thought I might go with him and Sylvie too, I'm not sure.'

'You always stop at Beirut on those cruises,' Evvy said enthusiastically. 'But it would be too tiring for you to take Sylvie, darling. Think of your nerves and *soignez* for heaven's sake.'

'Oh well, I'm not sure,' Alice said evasively.

'And you and Robert still see a lot of John?'

'God yes, the whole time, we're going to Crossbourne this weekend, as a matter of fact.'

'There's something wrong with that house,' Evvy said reflectively. 'I'm not quite sure what. Perhaps because John's not married and yet it looks as if he had an invisible wife with all those flowers about and all those little boxes.'

'Nothing's ever right, is it?' Alice teased him. 'You always give me such horrid rows for not having flowers.'

'But you are someone's wife, darling,' Evvy said, giving her a fond, worried look. 'You can drop me first,' he added as the taxi made its way into Knightsbridge. 'I've come to the conclusion that that astrologer is a fraud. I'm going to tell Ruth about her all the same.'

'What could she do for Ruth?' Alice laughed. Evvy climbed out of the taxi in Pelham Place. 'It was so lovely seeing you, Evvy, and I think you look marvellous. Much much better.'

She waved gaily to him as she was carried away out of sight.

'Hooray, you're here,' John shouted as Alice and Robert and three of their children climbed out of the station-wagon in front of the house. Crossbourne was an eighteenth-century house with a large garden that swept away to a lake behind and there were several stables and outhouses. A man appeared to drive the Greens' car into a garage.

In the stone-flagged hall there was a circular table with a visitors' book on it.

'How did you come?' John asked Robert.

'Oh, via Cambridge as usual,' Robert replied.

'Dad yi hov bid troffic?' John went on.

'Ni, bat wa dad gut maxed ip on i fratfil occidant,' Robert said.

'An occidant?' John screamed. 'Hi trimotic. Ony-body hat?'

'Yis. Win mun kalled.'

'Gid.'

The two men stared at each other with affection. Alice said: 'That lovely silly language,' and strolled into the drawing-room to find a cigarette. The gramophone was playing loudly.

'It's the new Johnny Mathis,' said John. 'You

haven't heard it yet, have you, Alpie?'

'No, what a treat for the weekend,' Alice exclaimed. 'You aren't having a real weekend, are you, John?'

'Well a tiny bit real,' John teased her.

'Oh, no – who's coming?' Alice asked in a worried voice.

'I was only joking,' he told her. 'Kathy's coming down tonight and that's all. Possibly Ruth and Robin on Sunday.'

'So it's just us,' Alice exclaimed with relief. 'We can have charades tonight, can't we Robert?'

'Yes we can,' Robert happily agreed.

'Shall we go for a subtle bound in the garden before it gets too dark?' John suggested.

'Ugh, what foul ideas you do have,' Alice replied. 'All right, let's.'

They all three went for a walk down to the lake, skirting several clumps of coniferous trees on the way. As they were coming back in through the front door they heard the hum of an approaching car.

'Oh good, that must be Kathy,' John shouted. 'Stop, stop,' he cried, running down the drive and flailing his arms. The car stopped abruptly and a girl jumped out.

'You poisonous bundle, how are you, we're all going mad waiting for you,' he screamed and threw her up into the air.

'Halli, averybidy,' Kathy called as she was spun round and round.

'Halli,' Alice and Robert called back to her.

'Doesn't she look subtle today,' John demanded when they had rather breathlessly arrived at the front door.

'Terribly subtle,' Alice affectionately corroborated. 'Oh, there are the children, that must mean that it's tea.'

'Goody goody,' John sang. 'Let's go in and have it.'

'I've got the most poisonous idea for charades,' Kathy announced as they sat over the crumpets.

'Kathy, you really are a life-saver,' said John beaming. 'What is it?'

'I wouldn't dream of telling you,' Kathy said. 'I might tell Alpie.'

'Oh, do, while we're changing,' Alice said brightening. 'But I must tell you about the astrologer I went to yesterday.'

'Oh, what did she say?' John asked quickly.

'You went to a what yesterday?' Robert enquired.

'A woman called Mrs Clare, she said the most extraordinary things.'

'John, do you mind if I try out an experiment with your tape-recorder in the study?' Robert said.

'No, do. You know how it works. Go on Alpie. I want to hear all about Mrs Clare.'

Alice looked confused. 'I'll tell you later,' she decided.

'Heavens it does sound poisonous,' Kathy said avidly.

'It is rather,' Alice admitted.

'Let's all have baths and get dinner over and then we can get down to the charades,' John said briskly.

'What a subtle idea – we could have dinner early,' Kathy cried.

'But I do love dinner here being so late,' Alice complained. John nodded his head vigorously.

'We'll have it at the usual time,' he assured her. 'Anyway, we won't be able to drag Robert away from that machine in a hurry.'

'He has such a heavenly time with that machine,' Alice said fondly.

'It's definitely John and Alice's turn to go out now,' Kathy said. They were sitting in the drawing-room after dinner. Small glasses of *crème de menthe* were placed beside them on the sofa tables.

'All right, shall we?' John said. They left the room and crossed the hall to go into the study. Alice sat down on the sofa and John threw himself at her feet. He took hold of her ankle and began to kiss it.

'You will tell him soon, Alice, won't you?' he said in a muffled voice.

'Oh, it's so terrifying – ' Alice began.

'But you must,' he insisted. 'You said you would in September and now it's nearly Christmas. It just makes it all worse the longer it goes on.' John edged himself on to the sofa and started to kiss Alice's face.

'You're so lovely and I do love you,' she murmured into his hair.

'I know you want to,' John whispered. 'How can

we know how upset Robert will be? He may take it all much better than we think.'

'I don't see how he can,' Alice said reluctantly. 'Somehow he seems to depend on me so much for everything. He wouldn't even send his suits to the cleaners if he was left by himself.' She drew John very close and kissed his ear.

'But he might find someone else,' John suggested.

Alice looked sad. 'I don't see how he could,' she said.

John drew away and stared into the fire.

'I will, I will,' Alice cried. 'I absolutely promise you I will. It's been just as foul for me not daring to tell him and dreading it so. It all makes me so worried.'

'Oh, Alp, you mustn't be worried about anything. We'll be married immediately afterwards. You do look wonderful tonight, did you know?'

'You're younger than I am,' Alice recited dreamily.

'Now you're being silly. You know you look fifteen.' He squeezed her hand.

'Or even thirteen?' Alice said laughing.

'But honestly,' John said more seriously, 'I'm sure he'll give you a divorce.'

'Why should he?' Alice cried. 'And what about his parents? They'll be so upset.'

'They'll be furious with me too,' John reassured her. 'Think of all the summer holidays I spent with them and Robert before he even met you.'

'Poor John having no parents,' Alice said softly.

'So promise me that you'll do it in the next few days,' John begged her.

'All right, before Tuesday,' Alice said with a sudden burst of energy. John hugged her powerfully.

'Oh, you are so marvellous,' he almost shouted.

'Sssh,' Alice said smiling. 'You're going away on your horrid job on Wednesday, aren't you? And I do need to have you here for moral support when I do it.'

'I'm only going for two days to inspect the works. And then I'll be back and it'll be the weekend and you can come down alone.'

'Because Robert will have left?' Alice asked, sounding terrified.

'Yes, because he'll have left,' John said in a strong voice.

They embraced thoughtfully.

'I want you to meet Luke properly,' Robert said to Kathy.

'I expect I'd love him,' Kathy replied, draining her glass of *crème de menthe*, 'but Alice can't bear him, can she?'

Robert gave a reminiscent smile. 'I don't know why, but every time that Luke comes to the house he seems to do something awful to Alice. Last week he trod on her bag.'

'How ghastly,' Kathy laughed. 'That's my slight reservation about him too, Robert. He sort of picks his nose and does funny things with the food.'

'But you like the recordings I made of him reading Provençal poetry?' Robert pressed her.

'Oh, I think it's wonderful,' Kathy assured him. She got up and went over to peer at a china clock on the mantelpiece. 'They've been gone for ages,' she announced.

'Who?' Robert appeared to start from a reverie. 'Oh, Alice and John. Actually, I feel rather tired. Kath. I think I'm going to go to bed.'

'You're dead right,' Kathy said, looking like a tired child. 'Gad-nit, Rabot.'

'Gad-nit, Kothy.' They went up to their rooms.

CHAPTER FOUR

Alice and Robert's bedroom in Montpelier Square was strewn with tweed jackets and underpants and cashmere jerseys. They were dressing for dinner and were beginning to emerge from this chaos in a dinner-jacket and a black silk dress.

'I hope I told them all to change,' Alice said vaguely as she screwed a pair of diamond earrings into the lobes of her ears.

'Who's coming?' Robert wanted to know, searching for his trousers.

'Oh, I told Mario to press them,' Alice cried, noticing her husband's mounting tension. She ran to the house telephone. 'Mario, Mr Green's trousers, where are they? No, NO, trousers, yes, pantalones, that's right. Pronto? Well, please . . . Oh, thank you. They're just coming,' she told Robert triumphantly.

'Ah,' Robert said.

'Ruth and Robin are coming,' Alice continued, 'and Evvy. And Elizabeth and Tom. And who else . . . Oh, Sylvie of course, and Judith.'

'Robin and Ruth seemed in good form yesterday,' Robert commented as he waited for his trousers.

'They love coming to Crossbourne,' Alice reminded him.

'I must say, so do I,' Robert said heartily. 'It's one of the few places I really do like going to. Ah, thank you, Mario.'

'I hope they're all right,' Alice cried, 'he's never ironed anything before, you know.'

'They look a bit odd,' Robert admitted, holding them up to the light. He appeared to be counting under his breath. 'We're a man short,' he calculated.

'We can't be.' Alice held her hand to her head. 'I must have forgotten someone . . . Oh yes, Mark Guest.'

Robert looked surprised. 'With Judith?'

'Why on earth not?' Alice said sharply, and then said in a kinder voice, 'It's nearly over anyway, I think. And Ben's in the North as usual.'

'Ben and Judith must see very little of each other,' Robert commented.

A doorbell rang.

'I'm ready and you're not,' Robert announced as Alice began to wail. 'I'll go down and cope with them.'

Ruth paraded in front of Evvy, who examined her with a sharp eye. They were in her bedroom.

'We're late,' Robin's voice floated up the staircase.

Ruth made a face, 'Do you think it's really all right?' she insisted.

'You look as fresh as a May morning,' Evvy

replied. 'Bless you, darling.' They kissed affection-ately. Robin's footsteps sounded on the stairs.

'Coming,' Ruth screamed, looking rather flushed. 'Promise to talk to me at dinner, won't you, Evvy?'

'If I'm sitting next to you,' he teased her.

'You are a beast,' Ruth said, upset.

They got into the car, which Robin had brought round to the door. 'I hate going out on Mondays,' he said forcefully as he let out the handbrake. 'It makes one so tired for the rest of the week.'

'These Jaguars aren't very comfortable in the back,' Evvy remarked in a low voice. Ruth turned round and made a kissing motion with her mouth.

'It's not very far,' she consoled him.

'What's that?' Robin wanted to know. There was a short silence. 'Who's going to be there?' he asked.

'I rang up Alice and found out this morning,' Ruth said. 'Judith and Mark Guest.'

'That'll be something to watch,' Evvy said happily. 'I didn't know that Mark Guest was a friend of Alice's.'

'He isn't really,' Ruth said quickly. 'I think he's a bit traumatic.'

'What on earth do you mean?' Robin demanded.

'He's so real . . . I mean he's the kind of person who sends flowers and presents and appears with aeroplane tickets to places. It's all too . . . somehow too . . .'

'You sound just like Alice,' Evvy said as they drew up outside the house in Montpelier Square.

'But why didn't you tell me that someone was going to come and make a horrible mess on the dining-room walls?' Sylvie's husband wanted to know.

'Darling, he's not just someone, it's Evvy,' Sylvie cried.

'I don't care,' her husband said stubbornly.

Sylvie seemed at her wits' end. 'It isn't nearly finished,' she assured him. 'He only started today. You wait and see, darling, until it's ready.'

'I'd planned a large abstract on that wall,' he said moodily.

'Darling, that's the whole point – it is an abstract, don't you see? I thought, as we'd decided to have a modern house, what a gift from the gods that Evvy said he'd paint something. And we don't have to pay him,' she added.

'I don't care.'

'I think you're being very unreasonable,' Sylvie decided. 'Oh, darling, why don't you change your mind and come to dinner after all?'

'I told you last week that this week I would have work to do,' her husband said. 'Who's going to be there, anyway?'

'Ruth and Robin and Elizabeth and Tom and Judith and Mark Guest,' Sylvie recited, 'Oh, do change your mind. Alice isn't the sort of person who cares about that. Oh and Evvy,' she added in a lower voice.

'Then you'll have a lovely time, won't you?' her husband said. 'Le Highlife.'

He laughed.

Sylvie, in going out, slammed the door.

'If there's one thing in the world that I would like,' Elizabeth said as she finished making up her face in front of the mirror, 'it's Alice's house.'

Tom had had several whiskies and sodas downstairs before going up to see what was keeping his wife. Now he sat on a chair in the large bedroom with a fresh drink between his knees. 'We've only just moved in here,' he reminded her.

'I know, I know.' Eyebrows were pencilled in and very red lipstick over the mouth. Elizabeth took a Cartier evening bag that had been laid out for her on the bed and slid a gold powder box and comb into its interior.

'It's such a heavenly house, and one could do the most marvellous things to it,' she went on.

'Are you ready? Because it's late.' Tom said a little impatiently.

'Oh, poor Alice, we'll ruin her dinner,' Elizabeth cried. 'I rang her up and found out who's going to be there,' she added as they went down two flights of stairs.

'Oh, who?' Tom asked.

'Evvy. You know who I mean. They all seem to be mad about him, but I've never quite seen the point.'

'I quite agree,' Tom said. 'Who else?'

'Judith and Mark Guest, and I think Ru . . .'

36

'So it's Judith and Mark Guest now, is it?' Tom mused.

'You knew that,' Elizabeth said in a scolding voice. 'Mark Guest is the absolute end. I can't bear him being so conceited. I suppose that he is handsome and all that, but really – ' She broke off as they reached the doorstep. 'Shall we go in separate cars?'

'Yes, why not?' Tom said. 'Hope to see you there.' They laughed at the familiar joke.

'Don't you like it?' Alice asked Mark Guest, who had taken very little of the *bœuf-en-croute* that Mario offered him.

'I won't, thank you. It looks simply delicious, and so do you, Alice,' he said, turning to look full into her face. Alice blushed and stared straight ahead of her down the length of the table. She saw Robert, rather blurred at that distance, talking animatedly to Sylvie on his left. Judith, who was on his right, appeared to be deep in conversation with Evvy.

'You've hardly spoken to Ruth at all,' Alice said turning once more to Mark. She glanced sideways at her other neighbour, Robin, who seemed to be talking seriously to Elizabeth. The only silence at the table was between Ruth and Tom.

'I can't stand bores,' Mark confessed, looking down at his cuff-links. When his features were in repose he looked very handsome. He was deeply tanned all the year round and had a thin face and strong chin; it was only when he smiled that a hint of cruelty could be discerned. Alice looked from him to Evvy thoughtfully.

'Ruth isn't a bore,' Alice said in a low voice with a giggle.

'Awful common little woman,' Mark contradicted her. He caught Judith's eye from the other end of the table. Judith gave a mysterious smile and sat up straighter. She was wearing a red dress which made her pale ash-blonde hair seem almost white and in the candlelight her skin was a delectable pink. Evvy looked darkly complementary at her side.

'Have Judith and Evvy known each other long?' Mark asked his hostess.

'Oh, for years I think, but perhaps not particularly well,' Alice answered stiffly.

'I want you to have lunch with me,' Mark continued, laying a hand on Alice's lap. 'We don't ever seem to have got round to one another, do we?'

'Oh, I couldn't do that,' Alice said, laughing. She gave a worried glance at Judith.

'I've always thought you were lovely,' he went on softly. 'So many things seemed to get in the way. Why don't we lunch on Thursday, little Alice?'

'Things still get in the way, don't they?' Alice said in a teasing voice. She turned her enormous grey eyes on him.

'I don't know what you mean,' he replied. He also glanced at Judith. A soufflé appeared between them.

'Is your diarrhoea any better?' he asked Ruth, turning to his right.

'What on earth . . .' began Ruth, flushing and laughing.

Alice turned with a small sigh to Robin.

'I didn't realize you'd been so ill,' Judith said to Evvy. She toyed with a minute portion of soufflé on her plate.

'Oh, I'm really not better yet,' Evvy explained to her. 'I'm sure I'd be much more amusing if I felt *en bonne santé*. I feel quite finished, I know it's an awful thing to say, but I used to look so young and fresh and now . . .'

'You certainly don't look a day older,' Judith told him. 'Tell me more about your life in Portugal – it sounds so fascinating.'

'Well, I'm surrounded by beautiful things and that's terrible important to me. You should come out and see it, you really should. Yes, why don't you? I'm going back there in a couple of weeks probably, and you'd love it then. Stay till the lilies come out,' he added with a laugh.

'But you said you were just off to Beirut,' Judith reminded him with a little smile.

'Oh, I'd change my plans for you,' Evvy cried with another laugh. 'I'm quite taken with you, I really am. I know I don't make much sense tonight, it's the cold I caught here that's interfering with my culture – one of my little theories – but you seem to look so different, Judith. You really do look lovely, let me see, it's your hair. No it's not. You just look good enough to eat.'

Robert went over to the sideboard and came back with a bottle of brandy and a bottle of *crème de menthe*. Judith turned to him. 'Ben's so upset not to be here,' she said softly.

Evvy flushed and glanced across the table at Ruth. Her voice had become rather shrill.

'So I went to see this little woman,' she was telling Mark, 'and she gave me the most amazing chart.'

'You've been already?' Alice cried, who had also overheard.

'I hope she said that Ruth's halitosis would improve in the coming year,' Mark whispered in Alice's ear. Alice gave him a short slap and he looked very handsome.

'What did she say?' she called out to Ruth.

'She said that everything would go right – that I only had to touch something and it would go my way. The most marvellous year of my life, she said,' Ruth confessed. She glanced at Evvy, who looked away.

'How does my mural look in the electric light?' Evvy asked Sylvie.

There was a lot of laughter down the other end of the table.

'It looks simply tremendous,' Sylvie answered, seeming rather distracted.

'So we'll lunch on Thursday?' Mark murmured to Alice when the laughter had died down.

'You know I can't. I'm a married woman,' Alice rebuked him happily. At the same time she succeeded in catching Robert's eye. 'Shall we go through?' she suggested.

'I do hate it when the men take ages to come out of the dining-room,' Elizabeth drawled. She had managed to tuck her feet up underneath her on the sofa. Her large diamond brooch was sparkling very brightly. 'You haven't really finished the drawing-room yet, have you Alice?' she went on.

Alice flushed. 'I wonder when I'll ever get round to it,' she admitted.

'But it's such fun, you'll love it once you start,' Sylvie encouraged her.

'You're very lucky to have something like that to do,' Ruth remarked sourly. 'Ah, here they are,' she added with audible relief. Alice and Sylvie exchanged glances, then Alice remembered herself. 'Who would like to go upstairs?' she wanted to know. All the women went up with the exception of Judith who was found sitting quietly on the sofa by the men when they came in.

'A little bridge might be a good idea,' Robert announced. Mark sank on to the sofa beside Judith and squeezed her thigh.

'We promised to go on, didn't we?' he whispered in her ear. Judith gave a smothered giggle.

'Yes, I suppose we did,' she agreed. Evvy wandered about distractedly by the fireplace.

'Couldn't we all go to a night-club?' he

suggested, staring at Judith. The women started to come back down the stairs.

'What's all this about a night-club?' Ruth cried.

'Oh, I'd rather stay here,' Elizabeth stated, sinking down on the sofa next to Mark.

'You're in very good looks tonight,' he told her after giving her a perfunctory glance. Elizabeth tossed her head.

'Thank you kindly, sir,' she retorted. Mark and Judith sniggered and pinched each other.

'Let's listen to the gramophone,' Alice said as she came into the room.

'Why not?' her friends said in unison.

'They all left rather early, didn't they?' Alice said in a worried voice. 'I don't think the dinner was very good. Actually it was all Ruth's fault. She almost made a scene to poor Evvy just because he wasn't paying enough attention to her.'

'I think Evvy was rather taken by Judith,' said Robert astutely from the floor, where he was kneeling with his face in the machinery of the hi-fi set. 'But it's nearly twelve, Alice. I think it went on quite long enough.'

Alice sighed. There was a long silence.

'Robert, I want to talk to you,' she said.

All that was visible of Robert was his behind.

'What do you want to say?' he asked in a muffled voice.

'I want to leave you,' Alice said.

Robert crawled out backwards from inside the hi-fi set and reached the sofa. He looked rather red in the face.

'Have you found someone that you want to marry?' he asked her.

'Well, yes, I have. John.'

'I'm very glad that it's John,' Robert said slowly.

'Swear that you're not too upset,' Alice begged him in an agitated tone.

'Well, of course it will be upsetting,' Robert admitted. 'But I'm not sure that we've ever got on well, have we?'

'No, we haven't ever got on at all,' Alice cried. 'Isn't it funny to think that we never knew that all these years? But are you sure that you're going to be all right? Without me, I mean?'

'I'm rather fond of someone myself,' Robert announced quietly.

'Are you really?' Alice stared at him. 'Not someone too horrid, I hope.'

'No one you know,' Robert replied. 'I shouldn't think you'd like her very much, actually.'

'So could you possibly give me a divorce?' Alice asked him nervously.

'Well, I'll have to think . . . no, of course I will, Alp. I think that John is the best person in the world for you.'

'How clever of you to see that,' Alice said, her eyes filling with tears.

'You don't think I'm in control enough, do you?' Robert demanded. 'I mean, I'm so bad at organizing things and arranging treats for you. And John is a great organization man.' He looked a little wild.

'Oh, I don't know,' Alice said vaguely. 'You're lovely to be with, Robert, it's just as you said – John is my person.'

'When did you first realize that we didn't get on?' Robert wanted to know, excitedly crossing the room. 'I think I first knew it on our honeymoon, when you so obviously didn't like . . .'

'Oh, don't talk about it,' Alice implored him. 'No, I never did like it,' she went on bravely. 'It isn't your fault. Promise.'

'I know it isn't,' Robert replied a little smugly. 'But everything of that sort is all right with John?'

'Oh yes,' Alice said, gazing at the floor.

'I only asked because I feel very fatherly about you,' Robert assured her.

'Do you really? I never thought you felt that,' Alice said, looking up at him. Robert had never looked so tall and masterful.

'We're both tired,' he said in a kind voice. 'Don't worry, Alp, everything's going to be all right. I'll ring John tomorrow,' he went on, 'and arrange to lunch with him. Where shall I sleep?' he asked her, smiling.

'It'll be so cold in the other bedroom,' Alice said in a weak voice. 'You might as well sleep in the usual place.'

'Well, don't worry,' Robert told her, 'you're quite

safe.' He gave a hearty laugh. Alice looked very white and upset. 'Up we go,' he said, pulling her to her feet.

They went up the main staircase to bed.

CHAPTER FIVE

The sun was shining and Ruth's bedroom, with its mauve stippled walls and fluffy white rug looked more cheerful than usual. A collection of Reynolds prints, given them by Robin's father, hung on the wall opposite the bed and it was against these that Evvy stood. He looked exceptionally thin and nervous in a dark-blue blazer with gold buttons and very dark grey trousers.

'I can't understand what you see in Judith, you of all people, Evvy,' Ruth said in a petulant voice. 'She's so affected. You used to say that she was the kind of person you dreaded most.'

Evvy looked annoyed.

'But why take such a shine to her now?' Ruth persisted.

'If you really want to know, since my illness . . .' Ruth gave a little moan of sympathy – 'I've had to face the fact that I can't do all the things I might want to. I've got one interest left, it's something that's fascinated me all my life anyway, and that's' – he lowered his voice – 'people'.

'Yes, she is a specimen,' Ruth agreed in a happier tone.

'And, anyway, she makes me feel *méchant*,' Evvy concluded with a belligerent glare.

'And I don't?' Ruth cried pathetically. He was saved from having to answer this by the arrival of the female half of the Spanish couple with some more hot coffee and the simultaneous ringing of the telephone.

'Hullo?' Ruth gulped into the receiver. 'You don't mean it? When? Good heavens. Are you absolutely sure?'

There was a short silence. Evvy stared anxiously at the telephone. 'But how extraordinary. They seemed all right last night,' Ruth went on.

'Is someone dead?' Evvy cried. Ruth waved at him to be quiet.

'But how amazing. Is it for anyone else?' she demanded of the telephone. 'Oh, I see.'

Evvy went very white.

Ruth cupped the receiver with her hand. 'Alice and Robert separated this morning,' she hissed at him. He sank on to a small buttoned chair by the bed.

'All right Elizabeth, I'll ring you back in ten minutes,' Ruth cried. She replaced the receiver and sat bolt upright in bed. 'That was Elizabeth,' she explained. 'Alice's nanny has just rung her nanny and told her that Robert packed a lot of clothes this morning and left with them for the office. Then Alice said she wanted to speak to her and told her that she and Robert had parted and that she was to be very discreet about it.'

47

'Oh *mon Dieu*,' Evvy said slowly. 'What can she think she's doing?'

'So I asked if she'd said she was leaving him for anyone else, but the nanny had said she hadn't mentioned that,' Ruth continued incoherently. 'Evvy, isn't that fantastic?'

'She's committing suicide,' Evvy pronounced.

'Oh, no, Evvy, she'll be all right,' Ruth said forcefully. 'She looks so much younger and prettier than she ever did – you remember how dreadful she used to look when they were first married? And she looks lovely now – actually, come to think of it, there must be someone for her to look like that.' Ruth swivelled round to stare at her reflection in the mirror on the dressing-table.

'I wonder who it could be,' Evvy said self-consciously.

'Yes, she is a dark horse, isn't she?' Ruth agreed.

The telephone rang again and interrupted their thoughts. Ruth made a desperate face.

'I'll answer it for you, darling,' Evvy said considerately. 'Yes, hullo, who wants her?' he asked in a brisk tone. 'It's John's secretary,' he told Ruth.

'Oh, hullo, yes speaking,' said Ruth, grabbing the receiver. 'Oh, we'd love to, I think. Yes, please tell him that we'd be delighted to come.' She rang off and said in a disappointed voice to Evvy, 'Just an invitation to stay with John this weekend.'

'You don't think it's John, do you?' Evvy said reflectively.

'Alice leaving Robert for John?' Ruth said wide-eyed. 'How could she? He's so unexciting some-how. She has been seeing a lot of him, I know. But Robert likes him so much . . .'

'I hope poor Alice isn't too upset,' Evvy cried. 'One can't ring her if one isn't supposed to know, I imagine. Oh *mon Dieu*,' he added.

'It can't be John,' Ruth mused on.

'I must go,' Evvy suddenly said. 'I must go to that *maison odieuse* of Sylvie's and get on with the mural.'

Ruth gave a deep sigh. 'What about our shop-ping?' she demanded.

'On a day like this?' Evvy said, surprised. 'I'll probably spend most of the day with Alice. She's going to need some friendship,' he added gloomily.

Alice had to wait for ten minutes in the Mirabelle before John appeared. She drank a very cold pale Martini and watched the ladies meeting for lunch in their huge hats. John bustled in looking tired and busy.

'Well?' he asked her breathlessly.

'It's all right,' was all she could say. John threw his hands in the air and jumped up and down. Then he flung himself on to the banquette beside her. 'How terrifically subtle,' he shouted. 'Waiter!'

A waiter appeared.

'Two large dry Martinis,' John told him. 'Ugh,' he added, turning to Alice, 'why did I order that?'

'I know, it's a foul drink,' Alice agreed.

49

'So what happened?' John wanted to know.

'Well, Robert said he was so pleased that it was you . . .' Alice began.

'Did he really?' John modified his voice a little when he saw that several ladies were watching him with interest. 'And he said he'd give you a you-know-what?' he went on mysteriously.

'Oh yes,' said Alice. 'Oh, John, isn't it wonderful? He's got someone himself.'

'He can't have,' John shouted again, 'Who?'

'No one we know,' Alice recited. 'So he's not miserable or anything.'

'I can't believe it,' John said in a more serious tone. Suddenly he looked tired again. 'What's the next step?' he asked her.

'I spoke to my lawyer this morning,' Alice said brightly. There was a short silence during which both toyed with their glasses.

'And what did he say?' John asked her.

'Well, of course I've got to go and see him. Tomorrow morning. But he did say that we shouldn't see too much of each other because it's me that's divorcing Robert. I don't quite see why,' she added, finishing her drink.

'It's very simple really,' John patiently explained. 'Robert's meant to be the guilty party and that's why you're divorcing him.'

A waiter came up to them and said their table was ready. John looked relieved.

'Yes, he is the guilty party,' said Alice in an aggrieved voice as they stared at the menus. 'All these years while I was having the children and everything he was seeing someone else.'

'This is a very bad table,' John said sternly. 'I don't think I've ever been put here before. What shall we have to celebrate our engagement?' he said to Alice in a fond, teasing voice.

'Oh, how lovely,' said Alice brightening. 'Shall we have the little black lumps?'

'What a subtle idea,' John concurred. 'A pot of caviar, waiter. But the whole thing wasn't too traumatic? Your conversation with Robert, I mean,' he pressed her as the waiter went off to get the caviar.

'Well it was horrid having to say all those things,' Alice admitted. 'Why, do I look awful today?'

She dived for her bag. 'Yi lak livly,' John assured her, squeezing her hand.

'I feel ancient,' Alice moaned.

'Now cheer up,' said John in a vigorous tone. 'Look, all our worries are over, aren't they? And here come the black lumps. And aren't they clever, they've brought some vodka with it when I forgot to order any.'

'Ah,' Alice said, definitely cheered up.

'I must say, that's a load off my mind,' John said heartily, as he spread the caviar thick on a slice of warm toast, 'because there would have been a nasty frost at the works if I'd been a co – . . . I mean if I'd had to put on those black and white shoes.' He laughed.

'And you never told me that?' Alice cried.

51

'I told you, Alpie darling,' he said in his patient voice, 'that I'd leave the firm altogether to marry you. And I would have.'

'But that would have been rather traumatic,' Alice pointed out.

'Well, it would rather,' John smilingly agreed.

'It's really terribly nice of Robert,' Alice mused. 'Oh, he said he'd ring you today, I do hope he remembers. He's so vague.'

'No doubt this woman, whoever she is, will keep him up to it,' John joked.

Alice looked upset. 'I expect she'll be a much better wife for him than I was, if he marries her,' she said.

'There couldn't be a better wife than you,' John told her softly, giving her a deep look.

'Oh, you are a comfort,' Alice cried. 'I do hope I'll do everything all right for you. But you know I'm not much good at big dinner parties. Evvy always says that the house looks awful because I never have any flowers or proper furniture.'

'Evvy doesn't know what he's talking about,' John said with distaste.

'And Mario always does such ghastly things,' Alice wailed on. 'I can't manage him like Ruth does her Spaniards.'

John looked round the restaurant and recognized several friends. 'I've got a meeting at three,' he confessed. 'Isn't it a bore?'

They ate *lobster Newburg* in rather a hurry and relaxed again over the coffee. 'What are you going to do this afternoon?' he asked Alice anxiously.

52

'I think I'll go and see Sylvie,' Alice told him. 'I want to have a chat.'

'Be careful what you say,' John advised her. 'Does anyone know yet that Robert left this morning? He did leave, didn't he?' he added.

'Oh yes,' Alice assured him. 'I don't know if anyone knows or not,' she went on. 'Nobody rang me up this morning.'

'Well the important thing is not to mention my name,' John said firmly. 'We could get into serious trouble with the . . .'

'Oh, I wouldn't dream of it,' Alice said hurriedly as they left their table and made for the door.

Evvy was standing precariously on the top rung of a ladder in Sylvie's dining-room.

> '*Et maintenant, que vais – je faire,*
> *De tout ce temps que sera ma vie,*'

he sang.

'Evvy, do be careful,' Sylvie cried. She was standing watching him splash paint on the walls. Now and then a large glob rolled down the wall and on to the floor where she quickly cleaned it up.

'This brown and green is most *intéressant*,' Evvy assured her.

Two of Sylvie's children ran into the room. 'Oh what a naughty mess,' one of them remarked. Sylvie hustled them out to the hall and the au pair girl seized them to take them for a walk.

53

'They are the end,' Sylvie admitted despondently.

'I wouldn't like to have any *enfants* myself,' Evvy said from his height.

The door bell rang.

'Who on earth is that?' Sylvie demanded in an agitated tone. 'It can't be Harrods at this hour.' She ran out into the hall.

'Alice, how lovely to see you. What a heavenly surprise,' Evvy heard her say. He swayed slightly on the ladder.

Alice came into the dining-room. 'Gosh,' she exclaimed. 'You're here Evvy. It's beautiful,' she added, looking round her.

'Isn't it exciting?' Sylvie agreed exuberantly.

'You didn't ring me up this morning,' Alice accused Evvy.

'Oh darling, I couldn't,' Evvy protested. 'I was having such a terrible time with Ruth.' Alice laughed. Evvy looked down at her and they stared at each other hard.

'I am glad you've come,' Sylvie reminded her.

'I'm going to have a break,' Evvy announced, carefully climbing down. 'Why don't we all have a glass of *crème de menthe*?' he suggested.

'Oh yes, why not?' Sylvie said, opening a cupboard in the wall.

'For heaven's sake watch out!' Evvy screamed. A thin trickle of scarlet paint ran down the wall and spattered the inside of the cupboard.

Sylvie gasped. 'Oh, Evvy, I'm so sorry,' she said. 'I'll get a cloth.' She ran through into the kitchen.

'I want to see you alone,' Evvy said to Alice.

'I'm alone now,' Alice teased him.

'Let's go to Montpelier Square,' Evvy said, brushing this aside.

Alice shook her head vigorously. 'We can't leave yet,' she hissed.

Sylvie appeared with a cloth. 'I do hope the mural isn't utterly spoiled,' she moaned.

'I'll see what I can do,' Evvy promised her. 'It'll be finished by Monday, by the way.'

'As soon as that?' Sylvie cried in a dismayed voice. 'But how wonderful, Evvy. We can have the party on Monday night.'

'Then we'd better start inviting *des gens* straight-away,' Evvy said, yawning. 'Let's make a list.'

The front door opened and shut loudly. Sylvie was by now thoroughly upset.

'Who can that be?' she demanded.

It was Sylvie's husband back early from the office.

'Good evening,' he said drily when he saw them sitting on the floor of the bare dining-room.

'Hullo,' Evvy and Alice chorused faintly.

'Let's all go upstairs,' Sylvie suggested desperately when she saw him looking at the walls.

'We must go,' Evvy said quickly, getting to his feet. 'We'll plan for Monday then,' he said to Sylvie. 'Oh bother,' he added.

'What?' asked both the girls.

'The shops will be *fermé* on Monday and we won't be able to get good flowers,' he complained.

'They're not shut on Mondays in this country,'

Sylvie's husband said in a sour voice. 'What's all this, anyway?' he asked his wife.

'A party on Monday night for the *vernissage* of the mural,' Sylvie explained.

'Oh,' her husband said.

Alice and Evvy fled into the street.

'And now,' Evvy began as they got into Alice's little car, 'what exactly have you been up to?' Alice turned an anguished face to him.

'How did you know?' she wailed. 'Oh Evvy, wait until we're back in Montpelier Square. I can't tell you and drive at the same time.'

'Very well,' Evvy acquiesced.

They drove through the heavy late-afternoon traffic to Knightsbridge. Once in the house they made straight for the library and ensconced themselves in the two armchairs.

'Robert left this morning,' Alice said tearfully.

'But you told him to?' Evvy prompted her.

'Oh yes.'

'Then, Alice darling, what are you going to do?' Evvy wanted to know. He got up and walked over to the fireplace, looking very distraught.

'Well, I don't know,' Alice began.

'And what will happen to the house?' Evvy went on. His face was more haggard than usual.

'I've no idea,' Alice said truthfully.

'*Ecoute-moi*, Alice, do you think we could be happy together?'

'But, Evvy, we always have a lovely time,' Alice said, sounding surprised.

56

'You and Robert were never happy,' Evvy announced.

'Oh, could you see that?' Alice asked him anxiously. 'You're quite right.'

'We were wonderfully happy in Portugal when you came out, weren't we?' Evvy insisted.

'You were ill,' Alice remembered.

'Yes, Spain ruined my culture,' Evvy said reminiscently. 'But we're made for each other, Alice. A perfect *mariage*. And you'd be happy abroad,' he informed her.

'I do hate this country,' Alice agreed with vehemence.

'It's the first time I've ever proposed,' Evvy cried. 'You may think I don't look as young and fresh as I did, but if we lived in the Camargue for a little, I promise I'd get my health back. Oh, Alice, every drop of it. And I just simply couldn't live there by myself, I know I couldn't. And you'd make such a good sweet wife,' he said softly, falling romantically to his knees in front of her.

Alice looked very distressed. 'But Evvy, I didn't think you liked . . . well sort of . . . I didn't think you wanted to get married,' she finished lamely.

'Oh, I know I've held out. I've had such fun, I suppose. But I never imagined that you and Robert would part and you've always been in the back of my mind,' Evvy gabbled at her.

There was a silence while Alice searched vainly

in her bag for a cigarette. 'But the terrible thing is that I'm . . . well, Evvy, I'm going to get married already,' Alice confessed.

Evvy threw back his head and jumped to his feet. 'To John?'

'Well, yes.'

'You're mad, Alice,' Evvy cried earnestly. 'To that boor?'

'He's not a boor,' Alice contradicted him.

'Oh, my God,' Evvy whispered, subsiding on to the sofa.

'Honestly I'm sorry, Evvy,' said Alice, tearful again. 'But I somehow never imagined marrying you, you know I think you're the sweetest loveliest person in the world, but I don't think . . .'

'What?' Evvy groaned. He looked very beautiful.

'That it would be a success,' Alice admitted apologetically.

'Mrs Clare said that you would live abroad,' Evvy said stubbornly.

'Yes, but it made you so cross when I told you,' Alice reminded him. 'I knew at the time that you thought I was thinking of us,' she went on.

'I just felt frightened,' Evvy said almost inaudibly. 'Don't think there haven't been hundreds of people trying to marry me for years.' He sighed.

'Oh, I don't,' Alice cried. 'I think you've been so clever avoiding them.'

'I must go,' Evvy rose to his feet. 'I don't know when I'll see you.'

'Oh, soon, Evvy, for heaven's sake,' Alice begged him as he made for the door.

He sighed again and went out. Alice looked very tired.

CHAPTER SIX

When Evvy returned to Pelham Place he found Robin and Ruth sitting silently in their little drawing-room.

'Oh Evvy, you do look pale,' Ruth exclaimed.

Evvy went over to the drinks tray. 'May I take a drink?' he asked Robin in a facetious tone. Ruth giggled uneasily.

'Help yourself,' Robin told him.

'Sylvie's just rung up,' Ruth announced, 'and she hadn't heard about Alice and Robert. Do you mean to say that you spent the whole afternoon there and you didn't tell her?'

'Why should I?' Evvy answered distantly.

'I just thought you would have,' Ruth replied defiantly.

'When are you going to get the dining-room chairs mended?' Robin suddenly wanted to know.

'When the man comes to pick them up,' Ruth said impatiently, staring at Evvy.

'Daddy was rather hurt the other night at dinner when he saw they weren't being used,' Robin pursued.

'I'll tell Nanny to be in on Saturday morning in case the man comes,' Ruth consoled him.

'Why, where are we going to be this weekend?' said Robin, sounding interested. Evvy sat down stiffly on a chair in the 'L' of the room.

'At Crossbourne,' Ruth said.

'And Alice is going to be staying there?' Robin said in an ominous voice.

'I've no idea,' Ruth said airily, trying to exchange glances with Evvy.

There was silence, then Evvy said, 'It's most likely.'

Robin cleared his throat. After shaking out the contents of his pipe into an ashtray he remarked: 'Then I don't think we should go, Ruth.'

'What?'

'Robert is a great friend of mine,' Robin explained. 'And a business associate. It's up to us to stand by him.'

This time Ruth managed to catch Evvy's eye.

'Alice has been playing fast and loose for years,' Robin continued a little wildly, 'and if she's going to stay at Crossbourne this weekend, then we're not going.'

'Well really,' Evvy murmured.

'I see what you mean,' Ruth said quietly, not looking at Evvy, 'it would be sort of disloyal to Robert, wouldn't it?'

'Absolutely.' Robin banged the arm of the chair with his wrist.

'It's really rather disgusting of Alice,' said Ruth,

sounding as if she was talking to herself.

Evvy wriggled on his chair. 'Alice and Robert have never been happy,' he stated.

'A lot of people aren't happy and they don't leave their husbands,' Ruth said smugly. Robin frowned.

'Will you tell John tomorrow that we aren't coming?' he asked his wife.

'Yes I will darling, I think you're right.'

There was another silence and Evvy rose from his chair. 'I think I'll go and change,' he said defensively.

'I'll come up with you,' Ruth cried.

'I'm going to have a bath,' Evvy protested.

'Well then, I'll come in ten minutes.'

Evvy went upstairs. His hands were shaking by the time he reached the telephone in Ruth's bedroom. He dialled a number. 'Mayfair double three two four,' said a foreign voice.

'Can I speak to Mrs Defoe, please?' Evvy said.

'Wha?'

'Mrs Defoe,' Evvy repeated.

'So sorry, no understand,' the voice told him cheerfully.

'What nationality are you?' Evvy asked clearly.

'You want Mrs Defoe? Please wait a minute,' he was instructed.

'Hullo?' someone said softly.

'Judith, is that you?'

'Who's that?'

'It's Evvy.'

'Ah, Evvy, how are you?' Judith acknowledged.

'*Tu me manques*,' Evvy told her, 'can we lunch tomorrow?'

'I'm terribly busy,' Judith replied after a pause, 'but I'd love to see you. Evvy, have you decided which you'll do?'

'What do you mean?'

'I mean, are you going to Beirut or Portugal?' She gave a faint laugh.

'Oh neither,' Evvy rashly replied. 'What about Thursday then?'

'I'm booked up all this week for lunch,' Judith said in a stronger tone. 'Have you been to the Kokoschka exhibition? Because it's well worth going to,' she added.

'Oh I haven't, would you like to . . .' Evvy began eagerly.

'I can't,' Judith said, sounding faint again.

'I kept meaning to go,' Evvy explained, 'but I've never felt well enough, it's this cold I caught from Ruth. But I would like to see you, Judith . . .'

'You're still staying with Ruth, are you?' Judith asked.

'I'm thinking of moving to the Ritz,' Evvy improvised, 'because Jacques is a friend of mine and he always keeps me a suite on the park side.'

'That's a much better idea,' Judith said enthusiastically.

'You must come to my *vernissage*,' said Evvy.

'How delightful. Of what?'

'I've done a little mural in Sylvie's house and the party is on Monday,' Evvy told her desperately.

'*Dix heures*. You will come?'

'I'll try. Ben may be back from the North and in that case we'll spend a quiet evening,' Judith told him.

'It's a hundred and eight, Ladbroke Terrace,' Evvy insisted. 'Perhaps we could dine first.'

'I'm afraid I couldn't manage that.' He could hear Judith stifling a yawn. 'Look, my other telephone's ringing, I must ring off. But I'll certainly try to come on Monday night.'

'I'll be in the Ritz by then,' Evvy tempted her.

'My love to Ruth. Good-bye, Evvy.'

Evvy put down the receiver and paced across the room to the dressing-table. He sat on the little gilt chair in front of it and studied his face in the mirror. His perfect features stared imperturbably back at him. There were steps on the stairs and Ruth burst into the room.

'All my things have been moved,' Evvy complained without turning round.

'Oh, I'm terribly sorry Evvy, Carmelita probably put them in the bathroom,' Ruth apologized.

'Could you get them?' Evvy asked her.

'Yes, of course. Evvy, are you feeling all right?' she asked anxiously as she returned from the bathroom carrying several jars and silver-stoppered bottles. Evvy picked up the *collyre bleu* which she had brought him and squeezed an azure drop into each eye.

'The germ is *avec moi* again,' he admitted.

'Oh no, Evvy, how terrifying,' Ruth gasped.

'Shall I ring the doctor?'

'What's the point?' Evvy demanded in a self-pitying voice. 'My *Grains de Beauté* has disappeared,' he went on, rummaging amongst the bottles. 'Really, it's too much.'

'They can't have,' Ruth expostulated, 'Carmelita would never steal something like that.'

'Well, she has,' Evvy sauntered mournfully into the bathroom and the key turned in the lock. Ruth lay down on her bed.

Robin came purposefully into the room. 'Where did you say we were dining tonight?' he asked her.

'With the Becks.'

'The Becks again?'

'Well, it's you who likes playing bridge,' Ruth snapped at him.

'What has José done with my studs?' Robin went on.

'Probably stolen them,' Ruth said weakly.

'What?' Robin strode over to the bathroom door and tried the handle. 'And when will the bathroom be free?' he demanded in a menacing voice. Ruth buried her face in the pillow.

'It's horrible Wednesday. I do wish you weren't going,' Alice breathed into the receiver. December sun flooded the white-panelled bedroom and lit up the glass jar of marmalade on Alice's breakfast tray.

'I'll be back on Friday,' John's voice crackled. 'It really is essential that I go to the works. Anyway, you're going to have a busy little week, Alpie darling. It's the lawyer this morning, isn't it?'

'Yes, it is. But you will ring me from wherever it is that you're going?' Alice pressed him.

'Of course I will,' John assured her, 'there's just one thing,' he added, lowering his voice. 'Have you any idea where Robert is staying?'

'Why, didn't he . . .'

'Yes yes, he rang me yesterday afternoon and we're lunching on Monday. But there's something I want to ask him first,' he said mysteriously.

'He's staying with Luke,' Alice informed him.

'Ah, and where's that?'

'Do you know, I haven't the faintest idea,' Alice said after a pause.

'Never mind, darling,' John said after another silence, 'I'll see you at Crossbourne on Friday then. Come on the six o'clock.'

'Is anyone else coming?' Alice wanted to know.

'Well, Ruth and Robin were, but they chucked this morning,' John told her. 'Ask the lawyer if it would be all right for us to be alone there.'

'Oh, that would be much nicer,' Alice said brightly, 'I'll ask him.'

'Good-bye sweetheart.'

'Good-bye,' said Alice, sighing.

There was a rap at the door. 'Come in,' Alice called.

'A registered parcel's come for you,' said her nanny, handing it gingerly to her across the eiderdown, 'I had to sign for it.'

'Oh, thank you, Nanny.' Alice waited until the door had closed before tearing it open carelessly. It contained a red leather jewel-box from Boucheron and inside was a pair of black pearl earrrings.

'Gosh,' Alice gasped.

She held them up to the light and the bumpy black surfaces shone dully. Each was surrounded by diamonds which made a brave glitter. 'The darling.' Alice said aloud.

A note lay amongst the discarded paper and Alice picked it up. *'I can't lunch tomorrow as arranged so see you today at Wilton's. Mark.'* it read.

'But it wasn't arranged,' Alice cried, leaping out of bed. 'Oh dear, what shall I do? How worrying.' She stood absolutely still for a minute and then ran into the bathroom and turned on her bath.

When Alice returned from her successful interview with the lawyer she still looked very upset. She was just about to let herself into the house when a rather battered car drew up outside. It was Sylvie, who jumped out with her arms full of parcels.

'The Christmas presents for the children,' she shouted gaily. 'Can I come in for a minute? I hardly saw you at all yesterday.'

'And I haven't got your children anything,' Alice moaned, depositing the parcels on a chair in the hall. 'Yes, do come in, Syl, let's have a drink.'

She poured them both gins and tonics in the library.

'I thought that was a lovely dinner on Monday night,' Sylvie told her. 'The only person I was frightened of was Mark Guest.'

'Yes, he is frightening, isn't he?' Alice agreed with feeling.

'One somehow doesn't know whether he's going to be rude or terribly polite,' Sylvie enlarged, spreading herself comfortably in an armchair. 'Listen, Alice, I know all about you and Robert. Don't be cross,' she begged, as Alice began to make fluttering motions with her hands, 'I couldn't help knowing.'

'Did Evvy tell you?' Alice wanted to know.

'No, it wasn't him,' Sylvie allowed, 'but there's one thing I think I ought to tell you.'

'Oh, what?' said Alice terrified.

'That beastly Ruth,' Sylvie said heatedly, 'she rang me this morning and said that she and Robin weren't coming to Crossbourne this weekend because of loyalty to Robert.

'Good heavens,' exclaimed poor Alice.

'It's so ridiculous of her,' Sylvie continued, 'she said Robert was an intellectual and you weren't, and that you'd been playing fast and loose for years.'

'But that's not true,' Alice cried.

'I know, I know, and on top of all that,' said Sylvie, jumping to her feet, 'she said that it was I who had been a bad influence on you.'

'Good Lord.'

'I wonder,' said Alice's friend, 'why Ruth has

suddenly decided to adopt this high moral attitude. It's silly of her to expect any sympathy from me, after all I'm much more your friend than hers.'

'Is Robert an intellectual?' Alice wanted to know.

'I wouldn't have thought so,' Sylvie answered competently, 'but seriously, Alice, I think we all ought to teach Ruth a lesson. I've told Elizabeth, who says she'll warn Tom, and I think you might drop the hint to Judith yourself. Evvy of course will be on your side.'

'I wonder,' Alice said. She saw Sylvie looking at her curiously and went on, 'I don't see what we could do to Ruth that wouldn't make things much worse.'

'We can be cold to her,' Sylvie suggested. 'Very cold.'

'So everyone knows by now, do they?' Alice realized. 'Oh dear, supposing it gets in the newspapers. John will be so cross.'

'Then you are definitely marrying John?' Sylvie pounced.

'But if Ruth didn't know why did she chuck?' Alice pointed out.

'She just guessed.'

'Oh, then for heaven's sake don't breathe a word to anyone.'

'No, no of course I won't.'

The girls sat staring at each other for a moment. Sylvie said:

'And something very boring has happened about Evvy's party.'

'Oh, what?' Alice asked distractedly.

'That silly woman who organizes the Christmas Arts Ball rang me up this morning and said would I mind if it was held in my house. Apparently the Arts College or whatever it is isn't finished yet and so they can't give the party there. And the party's on Monday and lots of people have bought tickets so I couldn't refuse.'

'How absolutely awful for you,' Alice said. 'It's because you've got such a lovely big house,' she consoled her.

'I suppose there aren't many of that size,' Sylvie agreed, looking pleased.

'And after all it doesn't much matter what happens in it,' Alice said absentmindedly.

Sylvie rose to her feet. It's five to one,' she exclaimed. 'I only told you all that about Monday night because it means that one can't stop Robert buying a ticket and coming – or Ruth and Robin for that matter.' She made for the door.

'Shall we have a quick lunch?' Alice called as her friend reached the hall. But Sylvie appeared not to have heard for the front door slammed behind her.

It's terribly sweet of you but I can't accept them,' Alice said.

Wilton's was very full of pre-Christmas lunchers. Gigantic Stiltons were piled high on the marble counter and the pictures of feasting cardinals were bedecked with sprigs of holly. The proprietor came

70

up to the table where Mark and Alice were sitting, and some men who had finished eating pushed by, rocking their glasses of Chablis and causing the mound of brown bread and butter to sway precariously.

'Get out of the way, you fool,' Mark swore at him.

'Keep them for a little while,' he advised Alice casually.

'I really can't,' Alice explained. She was holding the red leather box tightly in her lap.

'Well, put them in your bag now.'

She did so and they sat in silence until the waitress brought two large plates of Irish stew.

'How's that common little woman Ruth?' Mark asked her.

'She's been rather unpleasant lately,' Alice said unwarily.

'Has she really?' said Mark, brightening. 'Do you think she likes me?'

'I shouldn't think much.'

'Do you mean it?' Mark cried, looking delighted. 'What have I done? Do you think she thinks I'm one of the handsomest fellows she ever met?'

'I expect she just thinks you're very rude,' Alice told him primly.

Mark beamed. 'And am I very handsome?' he pressed her.

'Yes, I suppose you are.'

'Better than that hideous fellow John?'

Alice stiffened. 'What's that got to do with it?' she asked him.

'I thought you were going to marry the lout. Could we have some more wine?' he called. Their glasses were filled.

Alice looked very pale. 'Whatever made you think that?' she demanded.

'Oh, I dunno, but I advise you against it. Fellow's a queer.'

'He is not,' Alice cried.

'Oh, isn't he?'

Alice looked thoroughly trapped while Mark continued to beam. 'Let's go through some of your other friends,' he suggested. 'What about that ridiculous Elizabeth Murray?'

'What about her?'

'Hear she's had her hair dyed blonde.'

'Has she? How do you know?' Alice said with interest.

'Oh, someone at White's told me.'

'She must look extraordinary,' Alice mused.

'I don't care what she looks like, but I do wish she'd leave me alone,' Mark said. 'Silly woman rings me up once a week to ask me to dinner.'

'Don't you ever go?' Alice asked him.

'Sometimes, but I really haven't got time for her.'

Alice looked both disgusted and pleased.

'Coffee,' she told the waitress.

'Which direction are you going?' Mark asked her when they had finished lunch.

'Oh, home,' Alice replied nervously.

'I'll drop you.'

'Oh, don't bother,' Alice cried.

A taxi stopped in front of them and Mark bundled her into it. 'I can't remember the address,' he said.

'Montpelier Square.'

'Good, please go to Montpelier Square, driver. Darling little Alice, I'm very fond of you, did you know that?'

'Oh, don't,' Alice protested feebly as he kissed her.

'Would you like to have dinner tonight?'

'No, I can't. What about your wife?' Alice asked him formally.

'Away.'

'Well, I can't anyway.'

'I'll come round at about eight,' Mark told her as the taxi drew up outside Alice's house. He left her standing forlornly on the pavement and waved cheerfully as he was driven away out of sight.

Judith's beautiful drawing-room was filled with lilies and Michaelmas daisies. The french windows at the back of the drawing-room looked out on to a garden which was very pretty in the summer. The tables were strewn with little boxes in extremely good taste and on the walls hung various delightful watercolours. She was sitting composedly on the sofa reading to one of her children when Mark strolled in.

'Run along, darling,' she instructed the child. It scampered out of the room.

'Have a nice lunch?' Judith asked her lover.

'Charming,' Mark assured her, 'little Alice is perfectly enchanting.'

'I've always thought so,' Judith agreed. 'She's so pleasantly childish.'

'Yes,' Mark said thoughtfully.

'I on the other hand had rather a dreary lunch,' Judith told him.

'With that brute?' Mark enquired in a casual voice.

'He isn't a brute,' Judith protested. She laughed.

'Why do you have to see him at all?' Mark said moodily.

'I suppose I quite like his company. I wish you wouldn't be so silly, Mark.'

'Are you sure that's all you like about him?' said Mark, sounding jealous.

'Of course. I've told you a thousand times.'

'Everyone says that he's your new lover,' Mark reminded her. 'And if he is, I'd like to be the first to know and not the last.'

'Honestly, what can I say?' Judith said, giving another of her attractive smothered laughs. 'And what about you, I'd like you to tell me. Lunching every day in Wilton's with someone different.'

'You know very well that Alice is the first one since. That woman Elizabeth Murray keeps ringing me up,' he went on, striding up and down the room.

'What again today?' Judith demanded in amazement.

'Well, not actually,' Mark admitted.

74

'Then I expect you're quite safe,' Judith said smiling at him.

'She's dyed her hair bright yellow,' he informed her.

'It's not true,' Judith cried.

'God knows what she must look like.'

'Pretty frightening, I should think,' Judith hazarded.

'I like real blondes,' Mark said, dropping on to the sofa beside her.

'Talk about people not leaving one alone,' Judith reminisced as Mark ran his fingers through her hair, 'that boring Evvy rang me again today.'

'Did he really?' Mark murmured, sinking his teeth into her neck.

'But he is very good-looking,' Judith said provocatively.

'Better looking than I am?' Mark sat up on the sofa.

'Well, he's a beautiful girl, so it's slightly different.'

'And I'm not'?

'You know perfectly well you're not.' They kissed.

'I thought we might go upstairs,' Mark suggested.

'Oh, did you?' said Judith, laughing.

'Yes, because I'm going away tomorrow for two days,' he lied. 'And then it's the damned weekend as usual.'

'Where are you going tomorrow?' Judith wanted to know.

'Taking the children out from school. And Ben must get back early next week, doesn't he?'

'Monday or Tuesday,' Judith replied in a quiet controlled voice.

'He's been away a lovely long time,' Mark commented.

'All right,' Judith said. They went upstairs to her pale bedroom.

CHAPTER SEVEN

It was Monday morning. Alice lay in bed. She was looking restless after spending the weekend alone in London on her lawyer's advice. John had spent the weekend alone at Crossbourne. Her nanny came into the room and said:

'You told me last night to wake you in time for your appointment.'

'Oh, yes,' Alice said, 'thank you very much.'

She got up and wandered dispiritedly over to the mirror. The black pearl earrings lay beneath it on the dressing-table. 'Oh, dear,' Alice muttered. She pushed her hair up behind her ears.

'Is there anything I can do for you?' the nanny wanted to know.

'No, thank you,' Alice said.

The nanny left the room with a disapproving expression on her face.

'Ten thirty at René's,' Alice reminded herself.

The telephone rang, but instead of answering it Alice went into the bathroom and locked the door.

'I wonder why that Christmas Arts Ball isn't fancy dress this year,' Ruth said.

'I'm glad it's not,' Evvy replied. They were sitting in the sackcloth room on the ground floor of Ruth's house. Evvy had given up visiting Ruth in the mornings before she got up.

'One day it'll be quite nice being in here,' Ruth remarked in a depressed voice.

'Do you think so? There's no light,' Evvy explained to her.

'Oh, how shall I get René to do my hair?' Ruth wailed.

'It doesn't much matter, does it? *Plus ça change*,' Evvy quoted.

'But it does matter. Mrs Clare said this was going to be my big year.'

Evvy laughed nastily.

'Evvy, whatever is the matter?' Ruth asked him earnestly. 'What's happened?'

'Oh, nothing. Actually, Ruth,' he went on, 'I think I'm going to move out today.'

'What?'

'I think I'm getting in Robin's way.'

'What nonsense,' Ruth cried.

'Well there you are,' Evvy said philosophically.

'Oh, Evvy, please don't move,' Ruth implored him.

'As a matter of fact I've got a suite at the Ritz.'

'Oh.'

'I'll tell you the *vérité*,' Evvy said, 'I can't stand your attitude towards Alice. I'm sure she minded very much that you didn't go to Crossbourne for the weekend.'

'But it was Robin that insisted,' Ruth said in a frantic voice.

'You agreed with him,' Evvy accused her.

'Well, perhaps I do feel that Alice played fast and . . .'

'You know she didn't.' There was a silence.

'I've packed my bags,' Evvy announced.

'All right,' Ruth said with sudden dignity.

'See you tonight.'

'Possibly.'

Evvy went upstairs to get his luggage.

'And who's going to pay Searcy's for hiring the things?' Sylvie's husband wanted to know.

'The Christmas Arts Ball will pay for almost everything,' Sylvia patiently explained.

'I see. And what about the food?'

'Look, for heaven's sake . . .'

'Well, I must go to the office. God knows what damage will be done to the house,' Sylvie's husband said. 'Not that it matters very much now that the dining-room's been made a mess of.'

'Good-bye,' his wife called, blowing him a kiss.

'Good-bye.'

'And how do you like your hair now that it's blonde?' the girl asked Elizabeth.

'I'm very pleased with it,' Elizabeth replied. 'I want the green shampoo and some hair-conditioning, please.' She leant further back so that her head was completely immersed in the warm water which the girl was pouring over it.

René's was very full and there was a long queue of wet-haired women waiting for René himself to set them.

'Who's doing your hair?' the girl wanted to know.

'René.'

'This way, please,' Elizabeth brushed her aside and strode over to René.

'Will it be soon?' she hissed at him.

'Two comb-out and a *mise-en-plis* and it will be you,' René assured her. Elizabeth made a face.

'Can't you manage it before?' she demanded.

'I will try,' René gallantly said. Elizabeth looked round to see if there was a free chair and saw Alice, Ruth, Judith and Sylvie. 'Hullo,' she grinned at them. They smiled at her. She remembered that Ruth was not to be spoken to and gave her a sharp glance. Alice and Ruth were unfortunately sitting next to each other. They sat looking straight ahead at their reflections in the many mirrors but were often pushed together by the bustling hairdressers. 'Madame Green *a l'air triste*,' René remarked to Ruth. Ruth looked away.

'Madame Lamont,' René's assistant intoned. Sylvie went over to him with a beatific expression.

'And what shall I do for you?' René asked her

80

pessimistically. Inadvertently Alice and Ruth exchanged glances.

'I sort of want it on top,' Sylvie instructed him.

'*Très bien.*'

'Mrs Defoe, you're wanted on the telephone,' said a girl, coming over to Judith. Judith went out to the receptionist's desk and cradled the receiver against her wet head.

'Hullo?' she said very softly into it.

'Judith?' said a man's voice. 'We're lunching today, aren't we?'

'Oh, Mark, you're back,' Judith exclaimed. She glanced quickly round her to see if anyone had overheard. 'What was it like in the country?'

'Wet. See you at one fifteen at Wilton's, my jewel.'

'Very well.' Judith went back into the salon and found that Elizabeth had taken her chair. 'I think that possibly I was sitting . . .'

'Of course you were!' Elizabeth brayed at her, 'but it's all right because I'm going over to René now.'

'Edouard will finish your *mise-en-plis*,' René promised the disappointed Sylvie, 'and I will give you the *coup de peigne*.'

'But will it look the same?' Sylvie pressed him anxiously.

'*Mais oui.*'

Judith took a golden acorn out of her bag. It turned out to be a watch, and after she had put it back she sat down with an annoyed expression in the chair that Elizabeth had just vacated.

'*A la grecque*?' René suggested to Elizabeth.

'Yes, please.'

Behind where the friends were sitting on their little row of chairs was a turmoil of angry women. 'I've been here for three hours,' one of them shouted. 'If one does have to spend one's life in this place then one ought to bring food,' said another wittily. René turned round and placated them by flashing a smile.

'It makes me so nervous sitting in here waiting for René,' Ruth confided to Judith, who in reply gave a restrained smile.

'*Et qu'est-ce que vous faites ce soir?*' René asked the girls.

'*C'est le* Christmas Arts Ball,' Elizabeth told him. René looked interested.

'Ah, it is a private ball?' he wanted to know.

'Not exactly,' Elizabeth admitted. Judith suppressed a smile.

'What are you wearing?' he went on as he bound Elizabeth's glittering hair over the rollers.

'Oh, just a perfectly ordinary little Dior dress.'

Again Alice and Ruth almost looked at each other.

'Are you going?' Judith asked Alice in a voice full of concern.

'Well I think so,' Alice answered evasively.

'It is slightly difficult for you, isn't it?' Judith insinuated.

'Oh, that part's all right,' Alice cried. 'I happen to know that Robert has bought a ticket. We wouldn't mind being in the same room at all. I just wondered if I would bother to go anyway.'

'It's always worth having your hair done in case,' Judith pointed out.

'I'm in no hurry, so do go ahead,' said Alice, blushing.

Eventually Judith's and Elizabeth's fair heads were placed under adjacent driers.

'Would you like the *Queen*?' Elizabeth screamed. Judith shook her head.

'No, thank you,' she mouthed, and took a paperback edition of Turgenev out of her bag.

An hour and a half later Elizabeth stood contemplating her reflection in René's mirror.

'I think it's superb,' she congratulated him as he built Judith's hair into a soft mound. 'Thank you very very much.' She turned to Alice, who was still sitting dejectedly in her rollers. 'What are your plans? We might lunch,' she suggested. Alice looked depressed. 'I'll never be out of here,' she warned her.

'Well perhaps I won't bother at all. I must just go and buy Nanny a *pâté-en-croute* and then I think I'll go straight home.' She saw that nobody seemed particularly interested and walked out to get her coat. Once in the taxi Elizabeth appeared to waver.

'I wonder where the best place for *pâtés-en-croute* is,' she said aloud.

'Where to, lady?' the driver wanted to know.

'Oh, Wilton's,' Elizabeth answered.

She arrived at the little oyster-bar and pushed

aside the plush curtain to go in. A crowd of people was clustered round the bar, and Elizabeth fought her way through them to ask in a bright voice:

'Do you have a medium sized *pâté-en-croute* by any chance?'

At that moment her sleeve was tugged by the old proprietor. 'Mr Guest is waiting for you in the next room,' he wheezed in her ear.

'Are you sure?' Elizabeth asked him in amazement.

'This way, please,' he yelled this time, and dragged her through the crowd.

'There must be a mistake,' Elizabeth desperately tried to tell him.

'Here you are, Mr Guest, sir,' the old man bawled triumphantly.

Mark looked up from his newspaper. His expression changed drastically. 'Good God, are we lunching?' he demanded. The proprietor lumbered away.

'No, no, of course we're not. It's the fault of that stupid . . .'

Mark began to laugh. 'He must have thought you were Judith,' he explained to her. 'Now that you've got fair hair,' he added.

'How extraordinary, we don't look alike at all.' Elizabeth said distantly.

'Sit down and have a drink,' Mark urged her. Elizabeth looked uncertain.

'Waitress,' Mark said. A waitress appeared and gave a comforting smile.

'Well, perhaps I'll have a glass of sherry,' Elizabeth said, seizing her opportunity. She sat down.

'What a pity I wasn't in when you telephoned yesterday,' Mark said.

'Oh, I only wanted to ask you about the school you send your two sons to,' Elizabeth assured him. 'Prep schools are so difficult . . .'

'Is your child as old as that?' Mark enquired in a surprised tone.

'No, of course not, but one has to put them down so early.'

'Nonsense,' Mark informed her. 'The schools are only too delighted.'

There was a silence. Elizabeth sipped at her sherry and looked as if she was about to leave. Mark glanced at his newspaper.

Outside, Judith was parking her car. She came into Wilton's and gave a sigh when she saw how full it was. The old man saw her and began making signalling motions. Finally he reached her. 'You can't go in there, Mrs Murray,' he told her, waving vaguely at the back room, 'Mr Guest's in there with Mrs Defoe.'

'What?' Judith cried. 'But I'm Mrs Defoe.' A lot of laughter broke out at one of the tables near the bar. 'Hey, what's going to win the three o'clock?' somebody shouted.

'Civil Marriage,' the old man shouted back at them and shuffled over to where they were sitting. Judith pressed on to the doorway of the second room. She saw in one glance Mark and Elizabeth at

85

a small table. Mark put down his newspaper and turned towards Elizabeth. He squeezed her arm. At the same moment he looked up and noticed Judith. She turned away and fought her way out of the restaurant, compressing her lips. They were quite white by the time she reached the street. Mark looked uneasy but continued to squeeze Elizabeth's arm.

'Stay and have some lunch,' he suggested.

'Well, actually I'd love some.'

Outside Judith got into her sweet little car and drove home.

'What would you like?' Mark asked her. 'It appears to be silverside today.'

'My favourite thing,' Elizabeth cried.

'Oh, look, isn't that Robert Green?' Mark exclaimed. Two men were pushing into the room through the forest of overcoats in the passage.

'And John,' Elizabeth said breathily. 'How fascinating.'

'We're going to have a good lunch,' Mark said, rubbing his hands together.

John and Robert sat down at the only free table which was just behind where Mark and Elizabeth were sitting. They both looked rather uneasy when they recognized their neighbours.

'Well, here we are,' Robert remarked in a hushed voice. John opened the menu briskly.

'Silverside, what a pity,' he commented.

Robert nodded in sympathy. 'I wonder if there's any dressed crab left,' he said.

'To get down to business,' John said in a managerial tone when a half-bottle of Chablis had been placed on the table, 'I think that most of the points can be left to the lawyers.'

'I quite agree.'

'But I do want to thank you for letting me have your lawyer. You're sure you have no hard feelings about that?'

'To tell the truth,' Robert said, 'I never thought much of him. Not that he isn't perfectly competent,' he added quickly. 'I just want to give Luke his first chance.'

'You're sure that's safe?' John asked him anxiously.

'Oh, absolutely, he's with a very well-known firm.' Two plates of smoked salmon arrived.

'I hope I make Alice happy,' John said.

Elizabeth nudged Mark.

'I hope so too,' Robert assured him. 'Dear Alice. We married too young, that was the main trouble.'

'I'm younger than she is,' John remembered.

'Not really.'

'What do you mean?'

'Alice is a real child,' Robert told his rival. 'She's never properly grown up. Delightful quality in many ways,' he added, looking pedantic.

'Mmmm,' John said doubtfully.

The last two portions of dressed crab in Wilton's were put in front of them.

'Well done,' John congratulated the waitress.

'There's one other thing,' John went on as they sank their teeth into the soft mixture. 'That's the jewellery.'

'Oh,' Robert said indistinctly.

'It is actually mine,' John reminded him. 'You know, when my mother died she gave it to your parents and of course when you married they gave it to you.'

'Oh, you mean the emeralds,' Robert cried.

Elizabeth leant precariously backwards in her chair.

'Yes, and I gave them to Alice. Yes, of course they're yours, John. We were just waiting for you to get married and then we were going to give them to you. And you are getting married,' he said with a laugh.

'Good. Sorry to mention it,' John said, looking uncomfortable.

'And where are you going to live?' Robert asked politely.

'Oh, I thought we'd live in my house.'

'I'm going to sell Montpelier Square,' Robert informed him. 'It's a very impractical house, you know. But Alice seemed keen on having it.' They signalled for coffee.

'I must rush home,' Elizabeth said to Mark with a rapt expression on her face.

'Oh, must you?'

'Will I see you tonight?' she wanted to know as she pulled on her gloves.

'At that party? Yes, possibly,' Mark replied

signing the bill. He saw a friend and went over to the other side of the room.

'Good-bye and thanks awfully,' Elizabeth called to him. She went out into the street after buying a *pâté-en-croute*.

CHAPTER EIGHT

Evvy's suite at the Ritz faced St James's Park. Three large rooms opened out of each other and in them heavily shaded lamps illuminated the stiff brocade curtains and the patterned carpets. On the Louis Seize writing-table stood a bottle of Krug 1904 which Evvy had obtained after a tussle with the wine waiter. He dipped it in and out of the ice-bucket and then flitted into the huge marble bathroom. It was ten minutes to eight. Evvy was dining with Sylvie before the party. Carefully he shook some *Grains de Beauté* into the palm of his hand and mixed them to a paste with water. He then gently rubbed it into his face. A bath full of scented hot water awaited him. 'I'll *mélange* the *Chypre* with some alcohol tonight,' he murmured to himself, 'and add some of the pure Indian essence.' He lay in his bath for a long time staring at his long elegant limbs until the water began to cool. 'Oh, this English climate,' he muttered, stepping out and wrapping himself in an infinite white towel. He dressed very slowly and then plucked a straggling hair from under his left eyebrow. The whites of his eyes a startling pale blue from the *collyre bleu*, he stood back to look at himself in the long mirror.

'*L'après-midi d'un faune*,' he said softly to his reflection and left his rooms after sniffing at a bowl of freesias on the way.

'Well, I don't know,' Alice's nanny said. Monday night was her night off and she sat with Elizabeth's nanny in the wide carpeted nursery in Elizabeth and Tom's house. Elizabeth's nanny was a good hostess and poured her guest another glass of sherry. She pointed to the *pâté-en-croute*, which stood on the table and was already half eaten. 'Have some more,' she suggested.

'Oh, I couldn't, thank you.'

Downstairs there was the sound of water gushing into the Murrays' two bathrooms. They were getting ready to go out.

'I don't know either,' Elizabeth's nanny said, 'we've just got ourselves comfortable in these nurseries. I don't think I could manage another move.'

'And very nice they are too,' Alice's nanny said admiringly. 'But what was it exactly that you heard them say?'

'Oh, it wasn't a question of eavesdropping,' her friend assured her. 'I was just passing their bedroom with the nursery tray – because it's Pont's night out – when I heard Mrs Murray say to Mr Murray "How high will you go for Alice's house?" '

'How high?' wondered Alice's nanny.

'Meaning money, of course,' said her wordly friend. 'Well, then I couldn't hear what Mr Murray said because he mumbles a bit in the evenings, you know.'

'Oh, yes, you told me,' Alice's nanny said sympathetically.

'But Mrs Murray said "I must have that house at all costs," and then I did hear Mr Murray say "I'll see what I can do." '

'What will become of us?' Alice's nanny cried in an agitated tone.

'Well, if Mrs Green doesn't tell you it's just as well to be prepared,' Elizabeth's nanny said darkly. 'Though she told you about the separation, didn't she?'

'Not till Mr Green had gone,' Alice's nanny reminded her dolefully. 'Oh, I'd hate to move out of my lovely nurseries.'

'Yes, they are nice, aren't they?' Elizabeth's nanny said, looking thoughtful.

'I'm sure Mr Green wouldn't dream of selling,' Alice's nanny retaliated.

'Poor Mrs Green won't have a penny now he's gone,' her friend pointed out. 'She'll never be able to keep up a place like that.'

The door opened and Elizabeth came into the room.

'Oh, Nanny, could you do me up?' she asked.

'You look quite lovely, Mrs Murray,' her employee cried. Alice's nanny modestly looked the other way while the back of Elizabeth's dress was being fastened.

'Isn't that a lovely dress?' she went on when Elizabeth had left the room. 'It's a Dior.'

Alice's nanny looked upset. 'I don't know how Mrs Green will ever get into her dress with only that proxy parent to help her,' she said sighing.

John arrived rather late at the party after a business dinner. A jazz band was playing and Sylvie's house was unfamiliarly dark. He groped his way through the front hall and as his eyes became used to the half-light he saw that the dining-room had a lot of people dancing in it. Small tables round the floor had each a red candle and several glasses. He could just make out Ruth and Evvy dancing together and he made his way towards them.

'Have you seen Alice?' he asked them indiscreetly. Evvy looked pained.

'They're in the drawing-room I think – I mean Alice is in the drawing-room,' Ruth told him. He received two violent kicks from the dancing couples as he left the floor. Once in the drawing-room, which was across the hall, he began to search vigorously. There was a big crush round the bar and on the sofas. Finally he spotted Alice in a far corner. She was sitting in an armchair and Mark was perched on the arm.

'Ah, there you are,' he cried as he reached them.

'Hullo, John,' Alice said, smiling at him.

'Can we dance?' John asked her. Mark got up and wandered away.

'Yes, if you like.' She gazed after Mark as he went.

They went back into the dining-room where Evvy's mural looked distorted in the leaping candle flames.

'I had a successful lunch,' John told her, beginning to twist.

'Oh, how did it go?'

'Robert was very helpful. He said that of course I could have the jewellery as it was mine anyway. Oh, you're wearing it, how nice. Well, darling, it's yours.'

'I thought it was mine all along,' Alice said, looking down at her emeralds. A twisting girl almost bowled them over.

'For heaven's sake let's have a drink,' John moaned.

They went back to the bar. While John was fetching two glasses of whisky Mark appeared at Alice's elbow. By the time John had struggled through the crowd they had gone.

Judith arrived with a large dinner-party. After leaving her coat upstairs, she wandered down and looked into the ballroom. Mark and Alice were dancing very close together. From time to time Mark kissed the back of Alice's neck.

'Is that silly bore going to leave you alone now?' he whispered in her ear.

94

'Oh, Mark, don't say things like that,' Judith heard her say.

Judith turned and went out into the hall. Here she bumped into Evvy who was crossing into the drawing-room with Ruth.

'Ah, *bonsoir*, Judith,' he said with relief. Ruth smiled at Judith ingratiatingly. Judith nodded at her.

'Let's have a drink,' Evvy suggested. They all three went to the bar. A waiter magically appeared with a silver tray and they helped themselves.

'I haven't had a proper chance to see your mural yet,' Judith told Evvy, 'but what I saw of it looked very pretty.'

'Why don't we dance?' Evvy said, 'and you can look at it then.'

Judith finished her drink and put the glass neatly on a table behind her. 'I'd love to,' she said politely. Evvy cleared his throat and looked exceptionally haggard. Ruth, who had an agonized smile on her face, was stranded by the bar. They joined the dancers. It seemed darker than before in the dining-room and Evvy found it difficult to explain the mural to Judith.

'I think actually it will be very *réussi*,' he told her. He looked incredibly romantic in the crepuscular light. Judith danced a little closer to him. Three inches away from them Mark and Alice were dancing and occasionally their backs brushed.

'Is Ben back from the North?' Evvy whispered in his partner's ear. Judith pulled away from him a little.

'Well, is he?' Evvy insisted, digging his fingers into her spine. Judith sighed.

'I haven't seen Sylvie yet, have you?' she remarked.

'No, I haven't. You know, Judith, I haven't felt like this about anyone for such a long time,' he told her.

Judith saw Mark lightly kissing Alice on the mouth and tightened her grasp.

'*Je t'adore.*'

Judith looked up at him and smiled appreciatively.

'I feel young again and I think my health is even a little better. If we never meet again I don't want to *oublier* this moment,' Evvy said in an impassioned voice.

'I'm sure we will meet again,' Judith said.

John was sitting at one of the small tables on the edge of the dance-floor. The atmosphere had become even more relaxed and he could hardly pick out Alice as she danced. There was a large furrow on his forehead. Sylvie's husband appeared and sat down beside him.

'How are you enjoying the party?' he asked bitterly.

'Oh, terrific,' John replied.

'In this light you can hardly see the mural.'

'I know. What a shame.'

'It's not as much of a shame as you think,' Sylvie's

husband assured him. 'What makes me laugh is that everyone had to pay three guineas to come here tonight,' his companion went on.

'But it's for charity, isn't it?' cried John, concentrating for a moment.

'That's the trouble.' For the first time the two men stared at each other. 'Anything wrong?' Sylvie's husband demanded in a casual voice.

'Oh, nothing. I couldn't be enjoying myself more.' He saw Alice and Mark leaving the dining-room with their arms wrapped round each other. 'Especially being in your lovely house,' John continued weakly.

'You don't seem to be in your usual form, that's all.' Sylvie's husband said with pleasure, 'Oh, here's Sylvie.'

Sylvie ran energetically up. 'I thought I'd sing some of my songs,' she said boisterously.

'Well, time I saw that everyone is getting enough to drink,' her husband said. He left the room. The band began to play a jazzed-up gavotte. Suddenly the room was flooded with bright lights.

'Sorry, that's my fault. I arranged it,' Sylvie said when she saw that John was blinking, 'but I do want to do my cabaret.'

'I'm longing to see it.'

'Oh, these lights are awful,' Evvy moaned, opening his eyes.

Judith also appeared to wake up and looked

round the dance-floor with a disconcerted air. 'I didn't realize there was going to be a cabaret,' she said.

'Perhaps it will be *amusant*,' Evvy said doubtfully. 'Oh, who on earth is that?'

'It's Sylvie, isn't it?' said Judith, peering.

'It can't be.'

It was in fact Sylvie, who had changed into a tubular silver dress. She appeared to be overcome by modesty.

'Shall I really?' she demanded of the dancers in general, who had cleared the dance-floor and stood in a semi-circle round it.

'Go on,' some of them yelled. The band started to light cigarettes and talk to each other.

'Well, I'll begin with a selection from *My Fair Lady*,' Sylvie announced. There was a faint hum of laughter from the audience.

If you asked me I could write a book
About the way you walk and whisper and look,

she sang in a curiously cracked voice.

'That's not *My Fair Lady*,' objected a voice from the back of the room. It belonged to Robert.

'Oh, nor it is,' she said, breaking off and giggling.

'Go on,' she was urged.

'All right,' she said and started again. Evvy drew Judith out into the hall.

'Let's go back to the Ritz,' he suggested to her. Judith appeared to waver. At that moment Ruth shot up and took hold of Evvy's sleeve.

'I must talk to you,' she hissed at him.

'Not now,' Evvy implored her, backing away. Judith raised her eyebrows.

'I think I'll go and get a drink,' she told him.

'Oh, I'll get you one . . . wait a minute, Jud . . .' But she had disappeared into the darkened drawing-room.

'Yes, what is it?' Evvy snarled at Ruth.

'Come upstairs into the little sitting-room,' Ruth begged him.

'No.'

'Oh, please.'

Evvy looked very stubborn and then sighed 'Oh, all right,' and followed her upstairs. Once in the little room, which had orange walls, Ruth flung herself on the sofa.

'Evvy, tell me what's wrong tonight,' she said almost in tears. 'Nobody's spoken to me or asked me to dance.'

'I danced with you,' Evvy pointed out.

'Yes, but not properly,' Ruth cried rashly.

'What do you mean, properly?' Evvy asked her in an ominous voice.

'Not like you used to,' Ruth went on obstinately.

'I expect people are rather disgusted with you after your behaviour over Alice,' Evvy suggested.

'But are you as disgusted as all that?' Ruth pressed him.

'I've been perfectly friendly.'

'Oh, Evvy, you haven't. Moving to the Ritz like that. I only wanted to show you how much I love you all along. I hate people who play games – I think if you love someone you ought to show them you do – we used to be so happy, didn't we? Oh dear, oh dear,' moaned poor Ruth.

'Look, Ruth, I'm very fond of you,' said Evvy, on whose face an unpleasant smile had appeared, 'but *vraiment* I think I saw too much of you when I was staying with you. You're not really attractive enough,' he went on, half to himself. 'That is, I don't find you terribly attractive. I'm sure lots of other people do.'

'They don't, they don't,' said Ruth, sobbing. 'Oh, Evvy, I thought you did.' She picked up someone else's discarded glass of whisky and gulped it down.

'You're drinking too much,' Evvy informed her. 'I wasn't expecting this at all,' he cried, striding round the little room, 'I don't feel well enough. I don't want to be *entrainé* at the moment. You're a very sweet friend but . . .'

'Oh, God, oh my God,' Ruth whispered to herself.

'I don't feel naughty when I'm with you,' Evvy said to her with a glint of triumph in his eyes. 'You'd make a perfect wife, but you're not naughty enough to be a mistress.'

'How can you say cruel things like that?' Ruth screamed. Her face was streaked with tears.

'Anyway, I'm sorry, Ruth,' he apologized, 'I honestly didn't know you felt that way.' Ruth got up and made her way brokenly to the door.

100

'Come, come,' Evvy said gently, going over to her. Ruth pushed him aside and groped for the door handle. 'Try and smile. Giggle a little,' he advised her.

'Giggle a little?' Ruth stared at him in amazement and gave a long shuddering sob. Evvy pushed past her and ran down the stairs to look for Judith.

Elizabeth and Tom had been together all evening.

'I've looked everywhere but I can't see him,' Elizabeth said for the fourth time to Tom.

'Perhaps he's in the ballroom,' Tom suggested a little unevenly.

'We'd better brave the cabaret and look.' Elizabeth noticed after making that remark that Sylvie's husband was standing just behind her.

'Isn't Sylvie clever to give such a wonderful cabaret?' she congratulated him.

'I've heard it before,' Sylvie's husband answered.

Elizabeth crossed the hall and came back with shining eyes. 'He's in there – at the back,' she cried.

'Can't it wait until tomorrow?' Tom demanded thickly.

'No, please, Tom darling, you promised.'

Tom made his way over to the ballroom.

Robert was wedged between two debutantes on the floor and was watching Sylvie with a contented

expression on his face. Judith was sitting with a
dignified look just in front of him. There was a glass
in her hand.

> *With a gu-hun, with a gu-hun,*
> *You can't get a man with a gun.*

Sylvie sang loudly. Tom fell over several people
before he reached Robert.

'Can I have a word with you, old man?' he yelled
at him.

Robert looked annoyed and then uneasy.

'All right.' He rose to his feet and followed Tom
out of the room, inadvertently giving Judith a kick
in the back. She stifled a cry. Evvy appeared in the
doorway and stared frantically at her. Judith caught
his eye and took advantage of the little path that
Robert had made to reach Evvy's side. They went to
get their coats.

'It's about the house,' Tom explained to Robert. 'I
thought you might be thinking of selling. And I
would definitely be interested.'

Elizabeth was watching them both from a safe
distance.

'Oh, well, actually I was . . .' Robert began.

'Without agents and all that,' Tom went on
drunkenly, 'we might make a little deal.'

'Er, yes, why not?' Robert appeared to ponder.
'Yes, I don't see why not,' he added, in a stronger
tone.

'What sort of price did you have in mind?' Tom
enquired.

'Good heavens. Let me see, I paid . . . Oh, no,' he broke off, remembering. 'Well I wouldn't take less than thirty thousand,' he went on in a business voice.

'Thirty thousand!' Tom exclaimed.

'For you,' Robert said cunningly.

There was a silence.

'Very well, that sounds reasonable enough,' Tom said slowly. 'I'll offer you thirty thousand.'

'Good. It's a lovely old house,' Robert told him. 'I know.'

Tom went over to Elizabeth and told her the news.

'Let's go to the Stork Room for a minute,' Mark suggested to Alice.

'Oh, I don't think I could do that,' she said, giving him an adoring glance. They were pinioned to the far wall of the ballroom by the audience. Sylvie was doing an apache dance and the spectators were trying to retreat, as much as possible.

'It would be so rude to get up and go,' Alice said thoughtfully. John, unable to come any closer, was watching her from the doorway.

'You love me a little, don't you, my precious Alice?' Mark whispered in her ear.

Alice looked as if she did. 'Don't marry that stupid fool,' Mark went on, glancing over at John.

'No, perhaps I won't,' Alice said unwisely.

Sylvie was by now lying on the floor and kicking her legs in the air.

'For God's sake let's go,' Mark said, looking disgusted.

John was out of sight for a moment and they slipped out without their coats and got into Mark's Bentley. They drove to the Stork Room.

CHAPTER NINE

Evvy's rooms at the Ritz smelt strongly of freesias. Judith, still wrapped in her pale fur coat, sat on the sofa. Evvy switched on the gramophone he had bought that afternoon.

> *Je te prenais pour un bijou rare*
> *Mais les bijoux comme toi*
> *Il y en a plein les boulevards,*

a man's voice sang softly. Evvy picked up a fresh bottle of champagne from the ice-bucket and poured out two sparkling glasses.

'I was drinking whisky,' Judith pointed out.

'Never mind, this is *délicieux*,' Evvy told her. Judith drank it docilely. Evvy jumped restlessly up and changed the record and the strains of a Chopin piano sonata filled the room.

'Oh, I do love this music! Oh, every time I hear professional playing I want to begin practising again,' Evvy cried. 'I'm working on a partita at the moment. But there's no piano in this apartment.' He looked discontentedly around.

'I didn't know you were musical,' Judith confessed.

'Oh, I'm not really, at least I suppose I am quite but I don't practise enough. It's so tiring and I haven't been well.' Evvy looked over-excited and feverish. He ran through the big double doors into his bedroom. 'Would you like to see my collection of scents and essences from all over the world?' he called to Judith.

Judith looked very surprised and walked slowly into the bedroom. Here a great bed lay under a canopy of yellow silk.

'I didn't realize the rooms at the Ritz were as nice as this,' she commented.

'This is *L'Herbe*, and this one here is *Arbre*, no wait a minute I don't think, it is, yes, that's right, and this one is *Caveau*,' Evvy explained, pointing to the array of cut-glass bottles on the table by his bed. He sat down on the bulbous yellow eiderdown and began to unstopper the bottles.

'And what are you wearing?' Judith asked him, sinking down at his side, and gently sniffing at him.

'Oh, this is a mixture of *Chypre* and an Indian essence, it's very banal really,' Evvy said modestly.

'It smells charming,' Judith assured him. Evvy jumped up again and ran into the next room to change the record. He came back holding the bottle of champagne and closed the doors behind him.

'Can you still hear the music?' he asked her earnestly.

'Yes, just.'

Evvy lit a candle in a tall glass candlestick which was on the table by his bed. He turned the lights off

106

at the switch by the door and climbed on to the bed beside Judith.

'Will you draw the curtains?' he asked her. Judith let loose the thick yellow curtains round the bed and they surrounded them and plunged them in gloom with a swishing noise.

'Why did you obey me?' Evvy asked her. Judith drew back a little.

'Because I feel like a rabbit with a snake,' she replied.

'Look at the patterns the candle flame is making,' Evvy said. He leant over and pulled Judith down beside him.

'Oh,' she said softly.

'Ah, you sweet thing, I want you so badly, oh, I feel as if there was no one else in the world, oh, how delicious, I could eat you.'

'Ah.'

'Oh, it's wonderful, I'd almost forgotten . . . you're so soft.'

'And you're very beautiful.'

'Oh, that's sweet of you. I do feel very young again and it's all because of you. Oh God, I love it, I love you.' The candle, subjected to a draught from the slightly open window, blew out.

'Ah, it's so dark and it's so deep and it's so wet,' Evvy cried.

A strong smell of freesias and *L'Arbre* and *L'Herbe* filled the little vacuum inside the bed-curtains.

'I think I'm going to . . .'

'Is it nice?'

107

'It's marvellous,' Judith said just audibly.

When dawn came it did not penetrate the yellow silk tent on the third floor of the Ritz.

Alice woke up on the morning after the ball with a splitting headache. She put out her tongue which was burnt from too many cigarettes and tentatively licked her cracked lips. A breakfast tray with a pot of stone-cold coffee on it lay on the end of her bed. There was the usual rap at the door.

'What is it?' she cried weakly.

Two of her children ran in. 'Why are you so late waking up this morning?' they demanded shrilly.

'Why, what time is it?'

'It's half-past eleven,' the elder of the two told her, 'and it's the end of term, we didn't go to school today.' Both children looked disappointed.

'I'll do something nice with you this afternoon,' Alice said in a feeble voice. 'Sorry, babies.'

'Is Daddy coming round today?' one of them wanted to know.

'I'm not sure. Now run upstairs and find Nanny.' Alice moved experimentally under the covers. The children ran off but five minutes later the door opened and Alice's nanny came quietly in.

'Mrs Green.'

'Oh, Nanny, could you come back later?' Alice groaned.

'Well, I'm going to be busy this morning,' her

nurse said in a brisk voice. 'And I'd like to have a word with you.'

'Oh dear, what?'

'It's about you selling this house and us having to move.'

'What?' Alice cried. She sat up in bed.

'Mr Green's sold the house to Mr Murray,' the nanny told her. 'I'm sorry, Mrs Green, but I thought you knew.'

'But when?' demanded Alice.

'Mrs Murray's nanny phoned this morning. Of course she knew that Mrs Murray wanted the house, but last night Mr Murray made an offer for it and Mr Green accepted it. Thirty thousand pounds,' she added.

'How do you know?' Alice moaned.

'Mrs Murray told her this morning,' Alice's nanny said accusingly.

'It must be nonsense, Nanny,' Alice said bravely. 'Well, at least . . . I'll see you later,' she added in a peremptory tone.

'I wouldn't like to move,' Alice's nanny warned her.

'I'll see you later,' Alice said wildly.

When the nanny had left the room, Alice dialled a number. John answered.

'Hullo,' he said in a businesslike voice.

'I wondered if you'd be at home,' Alice cried.

'Oh, it's you. Yes, I decided to work at home this morning.'

'Darling, I'm sorry about last night.'

'You did behave in an extraordinary way. Look, Alp, if you'd rather that we didn't . . .'

'Oh, no, I want to marry you so much. You're my person,' said Alice, throwing discretion to the winds.

'But you've been behaving so oddly,' John objected.

'I know, I know. I felt so strange after Robert left that I didn't know what I was doing. I must have been mad,' Alice went on.

There was a pause. 'Well . . .' John said with a sigh.

'Can we possibly lunch today?' Alice pressed him.

'I'm having a business . . .'

'Oh, John, you can't. Please, something so awful has happened.'

'What's that?' John wanted to know, still sounding doubtful.

'Tom has bought this house.'

'You don't mean it?' John said in a more interested voice.

'Yes, he has. And, John, I do love this house more than anything on earth, except you of course. I can't bear it,' Alice went on tearfully.

'How much did he pay for it?'

'Thirty thousand. The Murray's nanny told Nanny.'

'Well, well.'

Alice sobbed into the receiver. There was another silence.

'Perhaps I ought to buy it,' John said cautiously.

'Oh, John.'

'I'll see,' he told her in a condescending tone.

'Can we lunch after all?' Alice insisted.

'Very well, I'll see you at the Mirabelle at one.'

Alice arrived at the Ritz at half-past twelve and went down to the American bar. There was almost no one there and she sat down forlornly at one of the little tables. The barman smiled at her.

'Can I give you anything?' he asked.

'Oh, yes, I think I'll have a Moscow Mule,' she said, brightening. Mark came jauntily in. He bent down to kiss her cheek.

'And how are you this morning?' he said.

'I feel rather awful,' Alice admitted. She was looking very pretty in a white tweed coat and skirt and her hair was still extravagant from the night before.

'You look lovely,' Mark assured her. 'I'll have a Bloody Mary,' he called to the barman.

'Look, Mark,' Alice began. 'I'm afraid we can't meet again.'

'What do you mean?' Mark demanded. 'Aren't we going to have lunch?'

'No, we can't. And here are these back.' She opened her bag and took out the black pearl earrings.

'Don't be ridiculous.'

Alice appeared to be very upset. 'I promise you, Mark, the whole thing is too frightening.'

'What on earth do you mean, frightening?' Mark asked, looking thunderous.

'I don't know. It just is,' Alice added, staring at the carpet. Mark shrugged and leant handsomely back in his chair.

'Considering that we haven't even . . .'

'Oh, I know, I know,' Alice cried. 'But honestly, Mark, I can't go on seeing you.'

'Seriously, Alice, don't you like going to . . .'

'Oh, stop it,' Alice screamed at him, goaded beyond her endurance. She jumped to her feet. 'There's no future for us,' she went on in a quieter voice, throwing the little red leather box down on the table.

'What does that matter?' Mark said in an exasperated tone. He also rose and let a pound note flutter on to the table. By the time he had picked up the little box Alice was half-way up the stairs and he ran to catch her up.

'Let's just have one last lunch,' he suggested. 'Think of last week when I told everyone I was away and we went out to lunch and dinner for nearly three whole days.'

Alice's eyes filled with tears. She shook her head silently. They reached the top of the stairs and walked past the splashing fountain into the main hall. Mark suddenly stopped dead.

'Good God,' he muttered.

'What?' Alice followed his gaze and saw Judith walking slowly down the staircase. She held her evening bag in one hand and with the other was

112

firmly holding her coat round her. Mark stepped behind a pillar and drew Alice with him.

'Wait,' he hissed.

However, Judith was alone. 'What can she have been doing?' Mark said to himself in an appalled voice.

'Heaven knows,' said Alice, whose eyes were now dry. 'Oh, perhaps she was visiting Evvy,' she went on artlessly. 'I think Ruth was complaining to everyone last night that he had moved into the Ritz.'

Judith reached the bottom of the staircase and went out into the street. Mark dropped Alice's hand and raced after her. Alice decided to walk to the Mirabelle and turned round and left the Ritz by the other door.

POSTSCRIPT

It was mid-October. Alice sat in the library of her house in Montpelier Square. She was looking rather flushed. Upstairs a large children's party was raging and she could dimly hear the conjuror pretending to be a ventriloquist. The front door opened and shut and she heard footsteps in the hall.

'Hullo, hullo,' cried John, bursting into the room.

'Oh, hullo.'

'How's the party going?' her husband wanted to know.

'I've just been upstairs. It seems to be going very well,' Alice assured him.

John put down his *Evening Standard* on the sofa and went over to the hi-fi set.

'Is it working yet?' he asked impatiently.

'Oh, it's all my fault, breaking it yesterday like that,' Alice wailed.

'Never mind, darling,' John consoled her.

'Well, no it's not mended yet,' Alice told him. 'I waited all day for the men to come from Harrods but they never . . .'

The telephone rang. 'Yes, hullo,' Alice said into

the receiver. 'Oh, how are you?'

There was a pause. John sank on to the sofa and opened the *Evening Standard*.

'How lovely,' Alice cried. 'When is he arriving? Gosh, as soon as that? Oh, what fun. Yes, we'd love to, good, see you tomorrow then.' She rang off. John looked up expectantly.

'That was Ruth,' Alice explained. 'Evvy's arriving tomorrow morning from Athens and Ruth's got some theatre tickets and then we're all going to have supper at Sylvie's.'

'Oh, good,' John said.